The Dahlia Connection

The Dahlia Connection

Michael Dovell

12/9/95

Publications
Seattle, Washington

Though the characters in this book are fictitious, the Market is very real. There is only one Pike Place Market.

While still in manuscript, this book received honorable mention by the Southern Writers Association under the title *Askew at Arms*.

Published by:
SCW Publications
1011 Boren Avenue #155
Seattle, WA 98104
Phone: (206) 682-1268
ISBN 1-877-882-19-4

Printed in the United States of America
First Printing—November 1995

Acknowledgements

I'd like to thank all those who have supported my efforts in writing this book, especially Brian Dunn, my editor, his wife Nena, Michael and Ann Phifer, and Nancy Covert. Nancy, Ann and Nena were three of my readers who kept urging me on. Double thanks to Brian. This is our third project working together. Again, he displayed the patience, understanding and dogged persistence it takes to bring a project such as this into sharp focus.

Dedication

This book is dedicated to the people of Seattle's
Pike Place Public Market, for it is they—
customers, merchants, musicians, craftspeople,
hobos, and residents—who make this
wonderful market what it is.

Contents

Prologue

THE STRANGE EVENTS I'm about to describe, which changed my life forever, happened in one of the most magical urban settings I know of, Seattle's historic Pike Place Public Market. This amazing place—an open-air farmer's market, part carnival, part street fair—is one of the most powerful cross-cultural environments in the world. It's also one of the last and greatest bastions of good old-fashioned grassroots human endeavor.

Okay, okay. Maybe I'm prejudiced. It's true that I worked there a long time. But how many places do you know where both fish and dreams can take wing? In the Market they do. And that includes the dreams of barefoot, spoon-playing street musicians as well as those of well capitalized families with well thought out business plans. It's all possible.

But embryonic dreams are fragile and need protection. That's why I christened myself Fishmonger Emeritus and appointed myself protector of the Market. This proved to be a full-time, double-overtime job, and the only training was pure on-the-job. It was especially tough going because I'm a hang-loose kind of guy.

You see, I'd scarcely gotten started before I found myself embroiled in a mystery. It was initiated by a brief but intense love affair with Dahlia Swartz, a mysterious young lady who literally fell into my lap. Okay, to be absolutely truthful, I suppose I should reverse that statement. Actually it was me—all three hundred pounds of me—who fell into her lap.

As to my performance in solving the mystery, I have to say I failed. Failed in a big way. Chiefly because, before Dahlia, my synapses had become so loose that they were being used as rubber bands for the miniature slingshots tiny mind-cupids play with, randomly shooting them off, toying, teasing. Let me tell you: If left untethered, those little rascals can fuck up your brains big time.

But that's all behind me now. As you'll see, I did eventually rally my experiences and call them to arms. And today, at fifty-three years of age, my synapses are as taut as the strings on the late, great Charlie Mingus's bass fiddle.

But enough of this. Let me tell you about Dahlia . . .

Part I

Loose Synapses

Chapter 1

Topside

"Eh doo moppa, doo moppa, doo moppa, doo, doo . . ."

THE BRIGHT JUNE SUN was just peeking out over the Cascades behind the waking city. The light made me squint, so I turned away, reassuring myself that "it's better to be safe than sorry." At fifty I clearly understood that squinting caused wrinkles around eyes. I focused on Mount Rainier to the south.

Bingo!

I was struck in love again. She was bathed in pink from the rosy red sun. It caused deep shadows to ripple cleavagingly along her ample swellings. The shadows constantly changed their shapes with the sun's morning rise.

Miss Mount Rainier, I thought. It doesn't matter how many times you've been mounted, you'll always be a virgin to the next one in line.

I belted out to her in the passing wind, "Volare, ah, ah, ah, ah." Above me, spartan seagulls flapped and cackled a raucous response.

I had to admit, my normal early morning effervescence was greatly magnified because it was the first day I'd had alone since I'd met Dahlia Swartz three days ago. Time to reflect. The young lady had put a whole new topspin on my visions.

I glanced starboard as the ferry crossing's I-want-be-seen,

plump, purple-clad jogger purposefully tromped by on the rolling deck. I sniggered inwardly that, this morning, Her Floppiness was not going to turn me on for a second.

I got myself a young-un, I thought, yes siree.

We all swayed with the rhythms this grand, moving world of the good ferry *Walla Walla* was creating for us as she headed for Seattle. Her deep humming turbines lay down a reverberating bass line deep in the amplifying waters of Puget Sound.

I blinked in half surprise and turned. I could have sworn that my Miss Swartz was right by my side.

The thirty-minute commuter ride from Bainbridge Island was just one of the worlds I wanted to share with her. Regular riders share just a teentsy bit—tiny bit, dammit!—of the commute. Just a wink, a smile, a nod; that's all. Since I had served practically all of them at one time or another at the Market, I didn't mind questions about the price of fish or produce. I sniffed and thought how I had worked hard to make the most of my worlds, dammit, and it was time to start sharing them.

I steadied old red-cup-a-joe in the stiff wind, strained my neck muscles to their limit, and gave my best Look of Eagles to the gaggle of seagulls flapping and squawking around me. I chuckled to myself. Learning not to show your double chin—giving a "Look of Eagles"— was one of the primary rules of Hollywood.

"Only the focused survive," I yelled to them in a booming voice.

Several of the gulls flapped harder and jettisoned their loads in a philosophic gesture of solidarity. I nodded appreciatively. I was in awe of the birds. How did they always aim their crap downwind?

"Isn't nature marvelous?" I yelled, flapping my arms.

I usually come topside to allow my sloppy synapses to regroup, but I had discovered some tobacco I hadn't used. It was a special pipe blend sent to me by a Ketchikan colleague.

Drat, there I went again, affecting my speech even to myself!

Really. Old Ketchikan Pete was a drinking buddy, my mate, not a "colleague" for chrissake. I hardly knew him, 'cause we had shared Teresa for just one night.

Big old Teresa couldn't make up her mind who she wanted to spend the night with, so we had both staggered forward and volunteered for duty. We had all met at the Mecca Tavern, just a ways up from Ward's Cove. When the Mecca closed for the night, the fog and rain drove us into Pete's well-appointed camper and a night of getting to know each other. Pete had been commanding a Coast Guard cutter, and I had been pumping diesel at the public dock.

Focus.

Topside, I tried to keep my Look of Eagles as I reminisced, but when I took a puff on my pipe, I choked and gasped for air. I righted myself and looked at the pipe quizzically. I took another light puff, coughed again.

Focus! I said to myself. Well, really, old chap, you have a right to arrange your, er, demeanor. It's your turn to take charge. You are the captain. You're Deacon, Fishmonger Emeritus, who is now in love.

I smiled at the thought as I tapped Pete's stale tobacco out of my pipe. Again, for the umpteenth time, I explained to myself that I had gained my freedom with the help of a sizable winning lottery ticket that had allowed me to retire at the ripe old age of forty-five.

Well, fifty-one.

Damn! I can't stop shoveling the bull even to myself. And in retirement, no less! Okay, okay, I'm fifty-two. I pinched myself on the arm. "You are no longer Deek Davenport III," I announced, "you are Deacon Davenport, Master of the Pike Place Market!"

I used the pipe as a pointer and pumped it like I was lecturing a class of wide-eyed freshmen. The only one in earshot was the plump jogger in the purple tights spending the six-mile passage lapping the ferry boat, but she was wearing earphones. Hmm . . . who was she listening to? Tony Martin? Kurt Cobain? Pat Suzuki? I focused in on

the grunging movements of her torso. It had to be Snoop Doggy Dog.
I felt a twinge of guilt. Why? I snapped my fingers and hummed "Why
do fools fall in lo-ove? Doo doo . . . ooo wah, ooo wah. . . ." She
chugged out of sight, rounding the captain's quarters. I coughed,
turned back to my flock of seagulls and continued my lecture.

"The Pike Place Market is my world. The grandmother of them
all. Six hundred businesses. Thousands of moms and pops. Unbridled
human goodwill, enterprise and energy. It's my world. My world!"

A massive guilt blob moved center brain.

Will we get married?

I fought myself to ignore the question and turned and grinned
into the wind, remembering the consternation my name change
caused around the marketplace before WL. WL is short for Winning
the Lottery. Before that I was Deek the wisecracking fishmonger one
week, Deek the veggie vendor the next.

"I'm Deek. You remember me, don't you?"

How many times I've had to say that to someone who knew
me but ignored my presence. Deek the Geek. Again, I felt the guilt
welling up. What was it? Yeah, well—"Why do they fall in lo-ove."

It all had depended on how soon I got drunk or in a fight or
got some woman pregnant. Then I'd move on down the arcade to
another job, if I was lucky. A few years back I had to wait four months
for a gig. That's what it was like selling at the Market. Show business. "Theater in the midst." My papa called the Los Angeles Market
that when I was growing up in Santa Barbara. I've been playing the
lead role up here in the main arcade for years, just like my papa did
down south. The Main Man, that's me.

Another tidal wave of guilt rushed in. Did I get my little Dahlia
pregnant? No, no, not that; that's not it, I thought. She had told me
that it wasn't the right time of month. I know I went bright red in
the face when the gulls started to squawk in concern. I tried to sup-
press my guilt.

She has got to be older than sixteen, I thought. Of course she is, she's over twenty, she has to be. She showed her I.D. when she bought the two bottles of Beaujolais. But the guilt, sweet guilt. Just because I haven't been with a woman under forty in thirty years?

Yeah, I thought, I'm guilty of not being with a woman under forty in thirty years, that's it! Life can be so damn confusing.

I blinked into another guilt rush and shuddered. I tucked my dead pipe into its holder and zipped it up tight, then shook off the doubt and saluted Pete. "Up yours, Petie boy!" I spit into the wind and ducked. Boy, was his tobacco stale.

I turned and watched the spit wad barely miss the jogger. Its trajectory refocused my thoughts on the positive as the wad disappeared over the side, with five seagulls in hot pursuit. I blinked in amazement at their precision.

I regrouped my focus. I had figured that what had best prepared me for my new role was that I had played a lot of Scrabble, so I had a way with words. I mean, I had a big vocabulary even though I didn't quite know what all those words meant. Words sure had an effect at all the public meetings I had to attend in my new role.

"Words are a way of life!" I pronounced loudly to the gulls, which had turned again, flapping of their wings at my bellowing. "Besides, I have an overview, dammit!"

For the most part, I had lived at other people's homes in and around the beehive of the Market. Yes, the Market. She had saved me because . . . well, because she is so forgiving. Then, with the lottery winnings, a whole other side of my personality began forcing its way to the fore.

And now the capstone. Love.

Being basically a person who can't stand confrontation, I swirled around and looked over the side of the Walla Walla. A primordial rush urged me to escape: to jump and sink, or leap and fly. I gripped the railing and took a deep breath, then relaxed. I was giving into this onslaught of civility, synapse by synapse. I had given at least some order to this disgusting evolution going on in my brains. I had mapped out my objective almost imm ediately: protecting the Market's rich lifestyle. I snickered conspiratorially. I was a prime example of that lifestyle. I have self-interest, I argued. Self-interest. I love the market. I owe her.

I checked topside to see if I could see my reflection somewhere. After all, I was giving my best Look of Eagles. Unfortunately, there wasn't a shiny surface in sight. I shrugged my shoulders and relaxed.

Shaking the tinglings out of my arms I recalled, in the passing wind, that my first assignment as "Deacon" had changed my life.

🦂

It had come from a high-staller, Huey La Pomadoro, who had claimed to be related to a famous Oakland sculptor. Pomadoro . . . Hmm, that's Italian for tomato, and there ain't no tomato patches in Oakland. What some folks will tell you!

Huey's a high-staller, and high-stallers are the big cheeses of the Market, because all the big-shot chefs from the big-shot restaurants buy their fresh veggies from them. I saluted him and told him my set rate was ten bucks, which I would have donated to the Free Market Clinic if he had paid me. Huey reminded me that I was cheap, but that I was hired. He wanted me to complain to management that his chief rival was selling over-ripe melons.

So, naively, I investigated by donning a wig and acting like a customer, studying an over-ripe cantaloupe. The vendor quickly saw through my ruse and yelled at me.

"Deek, what in hell are you trying to pull?" He pulled the beak of my Buffalo Bill's cap so hard it dislodged my wig, revealing me to all the elements, not the least being his wrath.

"My name is Deacon," I announced sonorously, gathering myself up. This deep-throated pronouncement instantly calmed him. I continued by firmly explaining that cantaloupes could not be sold in such a condition. I then purposely plunged my thumb deeply into the stem of the 'lope and held it upright as if it were a pitted black olive. To my astonishment, this direct approach proved to be the way to handle the situation. The vendor humbly said that it would never happen again. He even called me Deacon.

I was—how should I say it?—elated.

"A buck thirty," he said.

"What for?" I asked.

"The 'lope on the end of your thumb, Deacon."

I slipped the 'lope off, dug deep, paid, and told him to keep it.

I rushed back to Huey to report my success, but he refused to pay me my tenski. He claimed his instructions were to report the incident to management, not to try to correct it. I finally figured out that Huey was using me to try to discredit his rival. I was angry, but not for long, because as I was licking the sweet overripe 'lope stickings off the end of my thumb, I realized that that was how I had been introduced to my gray-eyed, blonde haired Mademoiselle Dahlia Swartz, straight from the Arctic Circle.

That's what she said: "Straight from the Arctic Circle."

The rich aroma from my cup of Seattle's Best Coffee brought me back to real time. Mmm. I love SBC while riding the ferry. I held the coffee cup up and said, "Red cup, you're one handsome son-of-a-gun." I had an ulterior motive, since Starbucks was served aboard in a green cup, so I had to wave the red flag of my favorite brew. Well, those are the rules of the sea lanes along Puget Sound, dammit!

The plump jogger panted by, completing another lap, and I raised my cup in salutation. She smiled and gave me a high five. I turned and watched her big, round purple-wrapped rump. I swear she twitched her buns together just for me.

Ah, camaraderie on the high seas! What a wonderful volare—
er, morning.

Where was I? Where was I?

Focus!

Dahlia Swartz, yes!

❦

I had watched unbelievingly when she was literally thrown out
of a lime-green Lamborghini in which she'd been a passenger. The
machine had barely stopped when she flew out. The car continued
down Pike Place and got lost among the bulk and fumes of delivery
trucks.

Dahlia staggered backwards, tripping on a stack of pressure-
flattened cardboard boxes and landed in a highly compromising position, on her back with her legs spread wide, her skirt hiked up over
her face. Just inches above her tousled blonde hair yawned the gap-
ing mouth of the box-compressing machine, open and ready to flat-
ten her wonderful curves.

My upper lip started to sweat as I remembered that around her
corrugated plinth stood three streetwise geezers, who obviously
knew a good thing when they saw it. They had laser-beamed in on
her little panties that covered her, um, goods. Thrusting out of her
tiny pair of frillies were shapely milk-pink legs, searching for a bit
of equilibrium.

On deck, remembering this, my tongue started to swell, just as
it did when I had jerkily rushed forward to save the young Miss
Swartz.

I hadn't been a moment too soon, for as her legs were testing
the wind, three pairs of seedy pants were lowered, exposing three
streetwise butts: two pink and one dark, dark brown. I grasped at
my own belt buckle in a primordial gesture of solidarity with my fellow man, but broke ranks and shoved them aside with my three-

hundred pounds of girth. "Buckle up! It's the law!" I shouted at them, with a tinge of possessiveness.

The varmints understood primal authority and quickly hustled off, grumbling loudly and tucking in their shirttails.

I quickly reached down, grasped her swaying ankles and gently guided her legs all the way down to the cobblestones. It was a mighty effort on my part. The trip down was led by my head, and I caught a whiff of her vitals. Oh my God, was I embarrassed. I wildly thought of how David Niven would have handled the situation.

However . . .

Oops, oww and ouch!

I had to assume she was now upright in a sitting position and trying purposely to rearrange her garment into place, because of the hard patting I felt on the back of my head. I mustered what dignity I could and, in very proper English, asked her to please help.

"The age factor, my dear," I said. "I'm not as agile as I once was."

She pulled me out with all her might, then hauled back with her right arm and slapped me so hard it snapped me out of my stoop. I began to explain about my weak vertebrae, but she laughed. Then she began to cry, grabbed me, hugged me, and wouldn't let go for what seemed like hours. We were both riding high on the euphoric fusion of her vulnerability and our inadvertent intimacy.

The toot from the ferry's horn announcing our arrival at the dock pulled me back to the present. The city's massive steel and concrete towers climbed high overhead. While at sea we were kings of the realm. In port we were but a dot on the 'i'.

I sensed a slight rushing of blood to my forehead. I laughed. All this mental, philosophical jabber was masking my true need of the moment. I couldn't move because I had a hard-on. Thinking about Dahlia had inflamed my instantly excitable Paul Bunyan.

You see, just after that incident three days earlier, Dahlia had become my live-aboard lover.

As I counted "one one-thousand, two one-thousand, three one-thousand," like a kid QB, I thought about her effect on me. She was drawing rave reviews from the earthy side of my nature, but my survival detectors were in a state of full alarm, sending piercing shudders of fear straight through my gut, shrinking old Paul from his full-flowering glory to a deflated balloon by the time I reached six one-thousand.

I shuffled protectively forward. Guilt had mentally turned the gangway into a wobbly gangplank over a sea of circumcision.

Chapter 2

Blind Spaghetti

"Wine, wine, wine all the time . . ."

WHILE I ARRANGED MYSELF for disembarking, I thought once more of how Dahlia was ensconced—damn, there I went again; I meant shacked up—aboard the Exacto, my converted tugboat abode, anchored smack in the center of Eagle Harbor on Bainbridge Island.

Why did I constantly have to reassure myself of my possessions? I tut-tutted. It was just a nervous twitch from my past, precarious existence.

Focus!

I glanced back at Bainbridge Island and continued my mental ramblings. I still had a weird feeling that Dahlia was at my side, so I gave my sloppy synapses free rein.

"Actually Dee—you don't mind if I call you Dee?" I said, looking back. I laughed at myself getting deeper into my act.

"Yes dear, I named the tug after Exacto knives. What? Well, I like Exactos; they're efficient. I carry one at all times, just like I do a felt-tip pen and other small tools. I got the habit from my pop. Pop kept all sorts of things in his pockets because he was an engineer."

I was about to answer her imaginary question about his age

when I realized he had been dead for over thirty years. That kind of took me aback and I shuddered a bit. What was I doing, going a little batty?

I shrugged. Why was I going on like this? I shrugged again at my thoughts. I guess this kind of personal repartee is important to us not-so-sure-of-ourselves types.

I coughed.

Focus, Deek—I mean Deacon!

I lapsed back into my thoughts. The *Exacto* was originally called the *Gratitude*. Perhaps I should have kept that name. Sort of fits me to a tee. She'd been built in Portland in 1917, all fifty-two feet of her. As the *Gratitude* she'd had a checkered past. She was suspected of rum running during prohibition, though that's highly unlikely since she's such a plodder. Still, on record, as a working tug she'd towed log booms most of her life. She'd worked the length of Puget Sound, had run aground off Port Townsend in the Thirties, and had flat out sunk in the Fifties at a dock on lower Lake Washington where she was wintering. Some drifters had snuck aboard and didn't watch the old-fashioned plunger toilet when they flushed it, and it had back-pressured, reversing the water flow. The lake water had come in and she apparently sank like the proverbial stone.

Though she was raised and restored, the sinking left kinks in her personality, that's for sure. Like the rudder is ever so slightly askew, so when underway you have to constantly adjust the steering or you just sail around in a circle. At least I don't have to worry about her going far if she's ever stolen.

I snickered to myself. It was funny; I'd found out about her sinking just before I bought her.

I looked up at two debarking ferry passengers who probably thought I was talking to myself. I pulled out a mini-Snickers candy bar that I keep in my pocket for these types of embarrassing situations, then winked at the toothy couple and waved the candy. They looked a bit askew—damn, I mean worried—then laughed and accepted the candy bar.

I pulled out another and gave it to the woman.

"And one for the lovely lady," I said.

They moved on and I lapsed back into guilt mode because the candy bars were left over from last year's Halloween.

Talk about shelf life.

I watched them rip open the bars and take bites. I guess they were still fresh.

The gulls overhead wailed their disappointment at being ignored because I usually fed them a Snickers on my cross-sound journey.

Well, where was I? Oh, yes. An old dock codger had stopped while I was admiring the tug and asked if it was the old tug that had sunk.

I remember saying, "Wrong boat, fella."

"Yup," he'd replied firmly, with a smile. "It's the one. I was debarnaclizing this here Chris Craft in the yard when I saw her sink. Four street rats and a suburban dowager popped out of the window and skeedaddled to Seattle. Early mornin', it was . . ."

I laughed, remembering that the codger had moved on while I mentally subtracted ten thou from the asking price.

I saw the codger a month after the deal was done and gave him a hundred. He scratched his head, rolled the bill up expertly, and stuck it behind his ear. He looked at me like I had a screw loose.

"Never look a gift horse in the mouth," he said sagely, swinging on in his cocky, sailor-swagger sort of way. I had wanted to belt out the Popeye the Sailor Man song, but instead popped some shelled peanuts in my mouth. I remember him looking back over his seesawing shoulder. I had wanted to explain, but I let him have his fun.

Well, these recollections were successful in keeping old Paul at half-mast, so I stepped up onto the gangway.

"Never, never question the power of recollections," I mumbled, as my tongue searched between my teeth for peanut skins.

Several commuters looked blankly at me, but one guy in sunglasses nodded sagely. I had a big mental flash: Why the hell was my tongue searching for peanut skins?

As I inched forward in the thick mass of commuters, I thought of how little Dahlia had told me about her life. She had been running with fast, hot-tempered company, that's for sure. She seemed so young, so innocent, but had said emptily that it hadn't been the first time she'd been "kicked around."

This time, she'd actually escaped from the back-handing she'd been getting from "Slime Green Ricci Lamborghini" because he'd tossed her out of the car. While he was driving, no less.

A slick East Coaster. She didn't even know his last name. She wouldn't elaborate on what little she told me, because she was convinced he would beat her again.

I was wary because she had called him slick and handsome, and had had a far-away look in her eyes this morning just before I left her. I had told her flatly to stay aboard for a few more days. My concern was the large black and blue marks on her back. She had reluctantly admitted that Ricci had given them to her.

She had been slapped after she told him that she knew that some street artists she had met in Ohio were based in the Market. Ricci had told her, when they first arrived, to never contact the artists. He was a jealous type, because when she mentioned them a second time, she got slapped for that, too.

This was all part of a fantastic story about his "intense love" for her that she told me in scatter-shot fashion throughout our passionate first night, a bizarre tale about nasty fighting cocks, mounds of chicken shit and gangsters. He'd told her all this in the elegant confines of the hundred-thousand-dollar lime-green Italian sports car.

Stories that only a young person with no money and plenty of dreams would believe, much less retell in a teasing, cryptic sort of way. It had me worried, though, because she also assured me that she was over twenty-one.

Then again, she did have the bruises. They were very real.

In one way, I hoped she was telling the truth. I had no choice but to believe her. I wanted her; my Paul wanted her in the worst way.

We made love nonstop for three days. Ten times last night. Bullshit, just eight times. Bullshit, bullshit, bullshit!

This morning she said she was never going to leave me. Bullshit! Her whole story was romantic bullshit. But the urgency, the combination of need and innocence, the fear deep within her—she couldn't be faking that.

My thoughts were broken at mid-gangway by a large booming voice announcing over the loudspeaker: "Will the man who rides the red scooter please report to the car deck."

I looked up into the window of the waiting room, trying to collect my thoughts, when a hand thumped me on the shoulder.

"That's you, buddy," a firm voice said.

We both laughed. This wasn't the first time I'd done this.

I had to back up the gangway in complete opposition to the heavy flow of passenger traffic, causing lots of problems. The only consolation came from the couple who waved at me with half-eaten candy bars.

One of the last commuters I passed was an elegantly dressed lady I could have sworn had been wearing purple jogging tights just five minutes earlier. She winked.

I held up my hand and we exchanged dainty high fives.

I turned and watched her depart. I swear she twitched her big, round rump at me again, only this time it was swathed in a tight-fitting business suit, the kind that makes the girls look so appealing these days, especially the plump ones, their perfume carried by the dense scent of wool—smelling so good.

Ah, well. Once it was eye contact; now it's rump contact . . .

I hurried down to the car deck. Two deckhands had just flipped a coin to see who was going to wheel off my scooter after all the cars had been off-loaded.

My scooter is a Honda 50. Actually, it's a 49 cc type, so I don't need a special motorcycle license. The point being that I hate to take tests. I get so self-conscious when I have to take them that I usually fail. It's weird. I've driven motorcycles for forty years, but I've never taken a motorcycle driver's test.

Wincing, I squeezed the small helmet over my head, nodded to the crew, and buzzed off the ferry, helmet chin-strap flapping.

I arrived at the Market in less than sixty seconds and parked in my usual spot under the clock in Post Alley, right in front of La Gala. Best bar in the country, after the Tosca in San Francisco.

My office was just around the corner at Bugsy's, deep down in the tunnel that arches over lower Post Alley. In years past this street was famous for the seamen's bars that lined it: the Victrola, the Rice Bowl, and the Hideout, to mention just three of the establishments. They catered to the seamen who came off the tugs, fishing boats and barges with six months' of paychecks. It was the duty of these places to make sure the work crews had a good time.

I straightened my neck, forced the helmet off and pulled out my "West Seattle Stetson." Whenever I put on this floppy white longshoreman's cap I consider myself officially on duty. Proudly, I went around the corner and almost bumped into "Blind Spaghetti," Post Alley's unofficial *New York Times* news vendor.

When buying from Blind, you always have to check the date of the paper he tries to sell you because it could be three days old. Bob Pasta is his real name. He didn't get his nickname because he's blind, but because he gets blind drunk.

I first met Blind on a drizzly morning at Fifth and University by the bank of newspaper machines in front of Brooks Brothers Clothiers. At the time, I was soggy and damp, trying to explain to the well-dressed guy buying a paper that the machine had jammed on me, and that I was entitled to one too. As I explained, an expert hand reached in and grabbed the whole stack.

"I'm the paper boy," Blind announced crisply, and whisked away with about fifteen fresh copies of the *New York Times*. He did it so expertly that the well-dressed chap, who had opened the machine in the first place, looked at me suspiciously, and we both retreated with no paper. Two days later I ran into Blind at Westlake Park, drunk and still clutching several papers. He even tried to sell me one!

Months later, after running into him a few times, I figured out what was happening. He would grab a stack of fresh papers, sell enough to buy a bottle, get drunk, and in his stupor still try to sell papers. At any time you could tell how long he'd been drinking by how old the papers were he was trying to peddle you.

I looked at the date of the issue he wanted to sell me. It told me he'd been on a three-day binge. He wanted fifty cents, but I negotiated him down to two bits. He said that'd be okay if I bought two. I said no, and he caved in when I flipped him the quarter.

I took the paper, reasoning that it would look good at my office to have a recent copy of the *New York Times* lying around.

"Gracias," Blind Spaghetti announced in perfectly enunciated Spanish.

I saw a tinge of worry in his eyes, like he also understood that he needed to dry out. I didn't want to give him fifty cents because it was close to the price of a pint of rotgut wine. I reasoned that no one else would be stupid enough to buy a three-day-old paper from a drunk in an alley, so perhaps he'd spend the quarter on a cup of joe.

Blind was an interesting individual. One day when he was stone sober he told me all about himself. What I recall is that he originally was a merchant seaman who went to college to study languages. His first job was with the State Department in D.C. Next the private sector, then a job as an overseas business advisor. He spoke several languages: French, Italian, Spanish, German, Russian, Polish and English. At least he had spoken them in his professional days.

He told me he'd been a heavy drinker all his adult life. I had thought that one through, because I like the hooch as well, so I guess it's okay. But drink finally got to him and his marriage. After the divorce a few years ago he developed a penchant for becoming blind drunk.

Blind's old office was just up from the Market in the Terminal Sales Building. During his early partially sober days, he hired himself out as a tour guide for foreign tourists at the Market. As his "bottle spells," as he called them, slowly took over, he had to rely on more esoteric methods of survival, because his ability to separate his languages diminished to the point where he began sounding like the Tower of Babel. If the Tower of Babel could speak, that is.

I smiled to myself. Blind must have understood the innate value of his rather unusual talent, because he took out a street performer's license from Market management after several of us regulars vouched for his "character." He turned out to be very popular. So popular, in fact, that one day a TV news team recorded his act.

That evening, sober and serious as a judge, Blind waited for the news show to be aired in front of sixty TVs displayed on a huge wall rack at Sears' First Avenue store. He had managed to get Shuggy, the evening salesperson, and an old drinking buddy of his to turn on every set to the same station. Many of us who had helped him through his more shaky days showed up after he invited us. The news show came on, and after an hour of reports about Seattle violence and Puget Sound mayhem, the attention shifted to the warm, old marketplace and the now-famous street performer who could garble along in seven languages.

It was a great show, and we all applauded, including many

shoppers who had stopped to watch. Unfortunately, all this attention was going to Blind's head. We escorted him protectively back to
the Market, then went our separate ways. Blind's reaction to his
moment of fame was to go on a binge, and he wasn't seen for days.
It was shortly after this incident that his nickname surfaced.

At first it was Blind Bob. Then Blind Baby Pasta. Now, one year
later, the nickname had evolved to Blind Spaghetti. As Chester Himes,
the late gifted writer would say: Bob went "from sugar to shucks to
shit" in a very short time.

I have a soft spot for Blind because he's a survivor. I found
myself thinking: Yes, I've got it. Blind will be the best man at our
wedding. Dahlia and he should get along just fine. They both exer-
cise a willing suspension of disbelief.

Now where did that come from?

The writer Coleridge. One of Grandpa's favorite utterings.

Or was it "Jingle bells, jingle bells, jingle all the way . . . ?"

Focus!

Chapter 3

Bugsy's

*"For she's my marshmallow mama, my sweet-tooth sweetie,
selling lollipop lies . . ."*

MY OFFICE IS LOCATED in Bugsy's Pizzeria. When I arrived, the owners were't yet there, but I knew they would be in shortly to prepare for the daily lunch crowd.

Lea and her son Antonio run one of the best pizza joints in the city. Absolutely no question about that. They're a most interesting team. Lea mans the cash register and Antonio is the cook. Lea's husband died a few years back, and Antonio entered the business after years of flower-powering it along the shores of the Great Lakes. Everyone was amazed at how he took to the discipline of running a small business so quickly. Now he is a quiet, successful pizza chef with a small ponytail.

They rent me a table in the southwest corner that I use as an office for forty bucks a month. The only stipulation is that, if the place gets full, I have to give up my space during rush hour or else order a pizza. Three months into this arrangement and I haven't shut down yet, but I sure have eaten a lot of pizza. Usually when I'm not doing any paperwork I just close the office down at 11:30 because the establishment—joint, dammit!—is always full by twelve.

Bugsy's is amazing because, though you enter from the covered cobblestone alley under the Market, once inside, after you move over to the windows, you find you are actually six stories above seamy Waterway Avenue, the next street down. Such is the Market's convolutedness. It's actually built on a steep cliff that rises straight up from the city's gritty waterfront. The views from my window are of a bay filled with working vessels of all sizes and shapes.

The ferry *Walla Walla* that I'd sailed on this morning had already headed back to the island. The sun-splashed Bremerton ferry was just arriving, her docking heralded by a bellowing blast of her horn.

I began setting up my office by opening the partition and arranging it around the table. Lea and Antonio always allow me to put it up to isolate myself from their own daily routine. The partition is an antique Japanese screen that William, a third-level antique dealer, sold me for twenty-five bucks. Scuttlebutt says it's very valuable, and that I talked him down in price to far below what he should have sold it for. He wanted seventy-five; it's estimated to be worth several thousand dollars. The honest truth is that I didn't know it was so valuable. I would have gladly given it back if he hadn't been so ornery about it.

Rumor has it that the bear of a man has a crush on me. He's even bigger than I am: six-eight and topping four hundred, with a flat stomach and a massive back. He's a pussycat, though, under all the makeup. He doesn't make up like a woman; that's not his style. He's a retired professional Hollywood stand-in who can make himself up to look like anybody he wants to.

With his powerful figure, William's specialty had been standing in for particularly short stars for fight scenes. When cowboy films bit the dust his career faded. After he went broke he just hitched up a Ryder, filled it with his family's antiques and headed for Seattle. Here, he took out a lease and opened his shop in the Market's lower levels.

He still moonlights from time to time for political commercials.

The screen, with its pale white panels and black frame, is handsome indeed next to the raw brick walls inside Bugsy's. William told me it came from an aristocratic house in Japan that had been destroyed during World War Two.

I unlocked the sea chest that contains my "office," so to speak, and proceeded to arrange my desk. Actually, the chest never saw the sea. I call it a sea chest, but it came from Boeing Surplus. It's a stout instrument box I paid five bucks for.

Opening the chest, I took out the old-fashioned 1930's-style brass phone that was my late pop's and plugged it in. It doesn't work, it just looks real good. Next, I put out a feather pen and inkwell I found at the Market's daily rummage sale, followed by pencils, legal pads, and my trusty, well-used Canon bubblejet word processor. Then I put on display the antique Remington typewriter given to me by Bob Houston, the late playwright. Bob lived his entire life in Hollywood, so I'm proud of the plaque on the machine that indicates that it was originally purchased at Hollywood Typewriters. Finally, I brought out a huge brass vase that had once been a horn from a USCG Coast and Geodetic Survey ship. I bought it as scrap at Pacific Iron and Metal, down on Fourth.

If I have time later in the morning, after the flower shops open, I buy a huge mixed flower arrangement to put in the horn. I always present it first to Lea for inspection, because after I close shop she inherits the bouquet for the rest of the day. The next morning, if it's still fresh, I find it on my table once again.

Well, I huffed to myself, with Dahlia joining my firm, *that* would have to change. I wouldn't want my girls getting jealous.

I felt a slight guilt pang in the pit of my stomach as I looked around. I had an uneasy feeling that Ricci would feel quite at home at Bugsy's. The place had a vaguely mobsterish, Al Capone kind of feel.

I picked up a matchbook from the table. The cover had a motif of a machine gun being held by a guy wearing a stingy-brim hat. I tapped the matchbook several times on the table, then flicked it into the waste can. I was ready for the day's business.

I brought out a folder from the small, portable filing cabinet that occupied most of the room in the sea chest. The folder contained a listing of all the Market meetings. Since Pike Place Market is publicly owned, the public must defend its ownership by attending meetings and contributing to proper decision-making by management.

As Fishmonger Emeritus, I consider it my duty to attend and contribute to these sessions as much as possible. So I studied the listings, and discovered that a Market Association meeting was starting in half an hour, upstairs in the Goodwin Library. I knew the merchants had a cause in keeping down their rents, so I decided I'd better attend.

A pecking sound at the window reminded me that I hadn't fed Georgette the Seagull. I walked over to the counter to see if Antonio had left any pizza scraps. He had. A blue plate with a half-eaten wedge of deep-dish pepperoni and cheese was waiting under a glass lid.

I removed the lid, took the plate and returned to the window, opened it and placed the wedge on the sill. Georgette stabbed her beak into it and tried to fly off. It was a weighty piece. At takeoff she sank several stories before she regained momentum and staggered off and up to her roost six floors above.

I looked down at the parking lot bordering Waterway Avenue. Next to the sagging telephone booth at the corner of the lot was the remains of another seagull with its wings splayed out. Its colors of gray and white contrasted starkly against the oily pavement scarred in black. I could see the tread of a tire that had run over the bird. I couldn't help but see it; it's track had picked up the red color of the bird's allotted portion of blood.

My synapses did the twist, from revulsion to how interesting the pattern was.

"Thank God you ain't Georgette," I muttered, as I rummaged through my sea chest for my camera.

The light wasn't good, but my old metal Canon would do the trick. I bent down, zoomed in and focused, then took several snaps. Taking pictures always made me tense. I put the camera back and took a deep breath.

Georgette . . .

Georgette was a case in herself. I had known her for years. In fact, she had once been a Market celebrity in her own right, when she had been known as George the Seagull. She used to come up to all the windows in the Market, especially the ones at Dunhill's Cafe, located deeper in the Market. She had literally trained a whole flock of gulls to cadge morsels at the Market's many restaurants. But the George moniker bit the dust after Bea, the bartender at Dunhill's, spied him feeding two fledgling gulls. George was actually Georgette!

Amazing how we stereotype behavior. My favorite gull, which hangs around the *Exacto*, I call "Israel." He's wild and won't come near a human, so I feed him by placing some bread on top of my cabin. He waits till I'm inside, then swoops down and eats.

I hadn't seen Israel in days, but I was still leaving bread out for him. I figured he was still around since the bread kept disappearing. I had showed Dahlia how to do it and asked her to feed him.

Israel had a "V" pattern in his wings that made him distinctive; the dead bird below wasn't him.

With a few minutes to go before I had to leave for the meeting, I picked up an envelope that had been placed on my table. It was addressed to me, and the return address read "Adelle Sanchez." Adelle was a woman I had known for many years at the Market. She was Filipino, a grand woman who made the best Spanish omelette I've ever etten.

"Hmmm—'etten'—I like that word," I said out loud, to anyone who may have heard me, as I ripped open the envelope.

Lea and Antonio came in, engaged in animated conversation. They saw me and waved. Lea called out that the coffee would be ready in a minute.

Mother and son were both hard-working Chicagoans and proud of it. When someone asks them the secret of their fantastic pizzas, they just point to the sign that reads simply "Chicago." Lea is petite, with close-cropped gray hair that makes her look like a contemporary movie star. Antonio is a big man with the gentle, penetrating eyes of a big-city survivor.

Where was I?

Focus! Focus, Deacon!

Oh yeah. Focus.

I looked down at the note from Adelle. Yes, Adelle. She was out of the same mold as Lea and Antonio. Hadn't I often seen her talking to her omelettes as she made them, just like Antonio talks to his pizzas, looking in, coaxing them on as they gurgled and bubbled in the ovens?

Sure heard her grumble a lot. And the fights with Alain! Poor Alain. Try as he might, he could never win an argument with her.

Alain was owner of the cafe where Adelle had worked. He was a dashing Pinot Noir—half French, half Algerian—who had been literally washed ashore below the Market when an old Spanish coaster, on which he'd been a cabin boy, was confiscated for running illegal Chinese into the country. Alain, it's said, jumped off the starboard side while the Feds boarded on the port side. As it turns out, the Midi's—the Mediterranean's, dammit!—loss was Seattle's culinary gain, for Alain was a whiz in the kitchen.

Heard it told that, like most of us free-wheeling sorts, Waterway Avenue almost got him. It's a real skid row if you get too deep into the bottle, on drugs or in a depression, or if you zombie out through lack of vitamins. The street's hostile gutters will pull you straight through their cast-iron grates if you don't keep it together.

The Midi. . . .

The name took me back to my old neighborhood in Montecito. I must have been six or seven. My neighbor friend's pop was a sea captain who sailed the seven seas. His mom always started out a conversation with, "Now when I was on the Midi. . . ."

Boy, she was something else, big and kind of roly-poly.

Alice—that was her name.

I had once crawled under her chair while she was sitting on it, and a whole new underworld was revealed to me. I had sensed that I wasn't supposed to be under there, and when she started to squirm and squiggle, I started sweating. After awhile, she got to bouncing like, and I got really scared. I tried to get out from under that rolling mass of female flesh, but I was transfixed. Eventually, she got to rocking her chair so violently that I thought I was going to be crushed. Then, all of a sudden, she stopped and sort of squatted there, as if she had, well, relieved herself, like.

Next thing I remember is her grabbing hold of my pants and hauling me out of there, panting.

"Okay, Paul Bunyan Junior, fun's over," she said. "Get the hell out of there!"

When she grabbed my pants she also got ahold of my weenie, which was standing at absolute attention. At that moment in my young life, my randiness, my erection, and the name "Paul Bunyan" were forever fused.

Ah, Mrs. Alice. . . .

Focus!

My fifty-year-old mind was wandering again, until an overabundance of saliva made me focus on my second-favorite subject.

Food.

I smiled.

I just eat to keep the blues away.

That thought was rudely interrupted by yet another.

Dahlia?

Damn! I wasn't gaining any mental discipline, I was losing it! I frowned. Now where was I?

I looked down at her note. Oh yes, Adelle.

Man, I loved her omelettes.

I frowned again and returned her note to its envelope. I looked down at my large stomach and wondered what percentage of my stored vitamins could be attributed to her delightful omelettes. . . .

Had to stop thinking omelettes! Even my synapses had started to salivate.

I looked down at Georgette's empty plate and firmed up my focus with a hard drum roll of the fingers, a snort and a small burp.

Focus!

After Alain had closed his cafe, Adelle joined the crafts line along the Market's north arcade, where she sold jewelry that she made by stringing tiny beads. Through this fragile way of eking out a living, she got her two daughters through college. Later, a bad rumor circulated that the managers of the Market were thinning out the craft line, and Adelle, for this chickenshit reason, was pegged to be hounded off the tables. For starters, she was much older than the other craftspeople. And then a rumor got started that she was not a true craftsperson.

It made me angry just thinking about it. I took her note back out of the envelope. It was a lined piece of school-kid's paper, as precisely folded as if she had been schooled in origami. But the typewritten words looked as though the machine's keys hadn't been cleaned in twenty years. The sentence structure was bad, 'cause Adelle's English hadn't improved much in all the time she'd been in the city. She'd never had to because of the city's large Filipino community.

I recalled her memorable arguments with Alain. When he was angry, he lapsed into French and she responded in Tagalog. But what was great was the language they berated each other with when they were *really* angry; it sounded like a sort of pidgin Japanese.

I donned my reading glasses and read:

Dear Shivvy (she called me that because I used my knife instead of chopsticks when eating peas). *The managers won't let me change my business to include aprons that I make with a sewing machine. They say I must handmake them. Shivvy, I'm seventy years old, my eyes don't see that well anymore. They are trying to steal my way of living away from me. Please help me. Your friend, Adelle.*

I sat back, took my glasses off, and reflected on how wildly colorful her aprons were. They were also quite popular, and the only way she could keep up with sales was by using a sewing machine. The originality displayed in her work was pure Filipino. It had to rank as a major cultural crime to deny Seattle folks access to her work based on some dumb, inflexible rule.

For a long time I sat there, looking at her sad letter. It made me angry, for I knew that the Market director, who was making a bunch of rules that didn't make any sense to our free-wheeling community, had a mother of his own whom he deeply loved. What the hell would he do if somebody treated his mother as he was treating Adelle? To me, it was the height of obscenity to disregard this small plea that meant the survival of a woman in her seventies.

I picked up my phone and dialed management. After three rings, beautiful Annie answered, reviving my spirits. I loved Annie's voice, and was just about to describe it to myself for the hundredth time, but I managed to focus on the task at hand.

"Annie, I must speak with Mr. Singe as soon as possible."

Annie answered in her sing-song way, "He's out of the office. I'll tell him you called. He should be back around three, so he'll return your call then."

We closed our conversation with me singing a bit from the immortal Midnighter's tune, "Annie had a baby, she can't dance no more; yeah, yeah, yeah, yeah; she got to stop 'n walk the baby instead of me across the floor."

Annie laughed, "You rogue, you. I'm gonna sentence you to the Politically Correct University! You're gonna have to do time. Your jailers will be twenty-year-old spinsters taking courses like 'Professional Victims, PMS 109'."

We hung up.

"Down with segmented personalities," I yelled out, laughing. I had never met Annie in the flesh. She sounded Southeast Asian with a French twist. Old Paul started to twitch.

Lea came over, fussing with a cup of freshly brewed SBC.

"Well, big cat, why are you always looking like you're stuck between angry and happy? I wish you'd learn to orchestrate your whims better. Getting harder to read you. You should learn to focus."

Chapter 4

Market Morning

"Spoonful, spoonful of sugar . . ."

WHEN I LEFT BUGSY'S, steaming cup in hand, I climbed the stone steps up and around a vegetable stall, then entered the main Market area. The air was filled with the early-morning aromas of fresh-ground coffee, fresh-baked pastries, and fresh, fresh veggies.

I did a complete three-hundred-sixty-degree turnaround. It was all the same. Fresh everything. Tonk was setting up his one-man-band rig. Nearby, a blues guitarist strummed a soulful Willie Dixon lament about "one spoonful."

Spoonful of what, I thought. Sugar? Dope? Sperm?

He sang, "Some people die for a spoonful. . . ."

Tonk looked like he was having a bit of trouble. His rig was quite complicated, and he had to take it out of his truck to assemble it. Once assembled, it sort of stood there, a spidery metal frame made up of collapsible drum stands and plastic tent-support rods. Harmonicas and horns draped from it, as well as cymbals. There was also a stand for a sax and a guitar. Behind the contraption squatted a big drum.

The blues man with his twelve-string droned on as I went through my usual mental checklist upon entering the Market from Post Alley.

First, I glanced back at my scooter parked in front of La Gala, then down the alley to where Charlie used to park his truck, which would have been overflowing with empty bottles he had collected the previous evening from the many restaurants in the Market. Charlie could tell you in a second the state of the Market's economy by how full his truck was. He owned two mid-Fifties Chevy trucks. Both had their own personalities. Some days, when his favorite blue one was cranky, he used the black one. Charlie died last year, but I will always salute his memory. He was a thin, sharp guy with bright, chipper eyes set in his deep dark face.

Next I waved at "Big John" at his station at the information booth. Once, Big John had witnessed a senior citizen being mugged after using the cash machine, so he, being retired, had stationed himself there as a guard from then on.

Finally, I patted the big brass pig—"Rachel"—on the butt. Rachel is a gigantic piggy bank, placed there to cadge change for the poor folks of the Market. There she stands, center stage, smack in the middle of it all.

I'm not jealous of all the attention she gets but I do have a rather unique relationship with her; I always get an instant hard-on when I come near her. Not from her; from the curvaceous fishmongeress who works part time at the fish house just across the way. She wears shorts under her long apron, so she causes quite a stir to us erotically bent types every time she bends over to scoop up a fish.

She knows what she's doing. It's a great show, and I've spent many a lunch break sitting astride Rachel's hindquarters watching the lady work.

This morning, for old times sake, I straddled Rachel once again and old Paul flared up. I sat reminiscing while a flock of tourists waited patiently for me to unstraddle Rachel so they could take some snaps of their kids on the pig. I was so in a zone that they finally just plopped their kids on Rachel's neck and used my back as a backdrop.

I felt sort of silly sitting there because the fishmongeress wasn't working that day, and, well, now that I'm Fishmonger Emeritus and in love . . .

My warm remembrances were rudely interrupted when my eye caught the flicker of low, rolling green. I couldn't believe it. A lime-green Lamborghini had just turned into Pike Place. Its grill looked like a shark's snout. As the car turned, I felt the vibrations of her twelve-cylinder engine.

The shudders I felt on the ferry's gangway returned. Big Paul quivered once and retreated like a frightened turtle ducking into its shell.

"Don't panic," I ordered myself. "You're just balling the guy's broad, and he wants her back. That's all. Nothing to get excited about. You've been in this situation many times before."

I sat stock still, sort of untwisting, like, as I watched the car slow down to let a group of shoppers by. I wished Ted were there to help me suss out the odds of two lime-green Lamborghini owners visiting the Market in the same week.

Both with New York state plates.

Ted is the resident Market intellectual who knows everything. He's low-slung like the car, but definitely not sleek; his brains are in his paunch. Feed him and he thinks; feed him really good, and he's positively a genius. That makes this whole food market his grand salon.

Ted usually joins me for a corned beef hash breakfast at Dunhill's, and the repartee is astounding. With three bites the population of Omaha comes rippling out to within ten thousand souls. After six bites, Indianapolis speed records are casually name-dropped. For him to give odds on the chances of two New York Lamborghinis showing up in the same week at the Market would take two heaping bowls of Zarzuela at The Crab House.

I blinked out of my calculations and back into reality.

As the low-slung car made its way down Pike Place, I caught a glimpse of Ricci's stunningly handsome Italian profile. Through the window his arrogance wafted out of the car's cockpit like some sort of invisible force. His presence instantly made me aware of my body's stoop. I involuntarily slid off Rachel and tried to stand up straight.

The car rolled past and I relaxed. I got very mad at myself.

"Who the hell does he think he is, Caesar or something?"

I quickly got my act together and tried to catch his license plate number, but a dirty black Aerostar van came in fast behind him. What was a bit unnerving was that the van also had New York plates.

"Damn! Ted! TED!" I yelled out.

Before I could jot down its license, another car merged in behind him. As the cars moved on down the street, I felt a convoluted sense of male pride in realizing that I had taken Dahlia from such a snappy looking guy.

I didn't notice who was in the van. I laughed, thinking that, from the size of it, it probably was the dude's wife and their large Italian family following him to the Market. How was he going to explain Dahlia to his old lady and his five or six kids?

As I sipped the last dregs of Lia's coffee, Dahlia's story returned in sharp focus. It was difficult to believe for many reasons. She was just too unsophisticated for Ricci. He was supposed to be a big-shot Mafioso East-Coast type of guy.

Check, I thought; there he was in the flesh.

So why did she say he drove through Montana, of all places? Scratch that idea.

Well, I thought, it's obvious why he picked her up and kept her. But then to talk so openly with her? A total stranger?

Ricci sure didn't look the type. It just didn't add up. She said he was supposed to be . . .

"Hey, Deek! You got a buck?" A harsh, cluttered voice slashed uninvitingly through my thoughts.

My concentration was broken by Vandenberg Billy, struggling up the arcade toward me, asking for a handout. Billyvan—as I call him—is another case of drugs stripping a person of his dignity. He had floated to the Market from Lompoc, California, a few years back. A former ranch hand on a tri-county weed farm, he had gotten caught up with the crop.

I dropped my cup in a waste basket as he approached. Upon arriving in Seattle, Billy had parked his van in a clump of brush in one of the crannies just off Waterway Avenue and gone to sleep. He had awakened the next morning to find his car stripped of all its tires, its mirror and the engine. That had been years ago, but Billy and the van were still down there.

Billyvan.

"Outside, okay, but not in the Market," I gently but firmly told him. I don't give handouts at the Market.

"That's the trouble with this place," I muttered to myself, trying to get back to my dominant thought stream, "too much going on!"

"Next time I'm hitting you twice, you know that?" Billyvan yelled back.

I arranged a tight smile and waved back, acknowledging his reverse raincheck. I moved on confused. So much going on. The aromas wafting out of Fat Baker's brought me back down to reality.

I call the place "Fat Baker's" because it must be responsible for at least fifty extra pounds of girth I've accumulated from eating their walnut-topped, Texas-sized maple bars. Like everything else in the Market, they're several times larger than normal. That's the charm and the bane of the Market, kind of like sinsemilla grass: creativity and vitality crammed in to the bursting point, larger than life!

Seeing Fat Baker's retriggered a primal reason for coming up to the main arcade: food. Did I want a maple bar? No! Now I needed one.

What was Ted's first point in his philosophy of life? Nourishment of the body begets nourishment of the mind.

I just had to stop!

Dahlia's story resurfaced as I watched Denise, the pert clerk, use both hands to pick up the huge pastry and carefully slide it into the bag.

Dahlia had flippantly explained to me that Ricci was personally overseeing the take from members of a syndicate of cock fighters. The fights were held next to chicken farms. She said they had visited dozens in Montana and Oregon. The farms were huge barnlike buildings housing endless batteries of hens. Dahlia's nose had wrinkled as she described the smell from the mounds of chicken shit. She didn't know Spanish, so she couldn't understand what the men workers were saying as they climbed among the hens, millions of hens just sitting in little boxes. She said they were stacked endlessly all the way up to the rafters. She recalled the bright shafts of sunlight playing on the rows like death rays. The hens were unable to move out of the harsh light and just laid eggs and squawked.

A short Latino guy, carrying a fighting cock, had walked through the huge coop, and all the hens had stopped squawking and started wailing at the tops of their gullets. Dahlia started crying and couldn't stop. Ricci got so angry that he kicked the guy carrying the rooster in the butt, getting him to hurry out of the coop. Then she said he backhanded her to stop her crying.

Weird. What the hell was eating him?

After things had quieted down, Dahlia said, Ricci told her that a fighting cock was worth a lot of money, and the idea was not to distract him with hens.

She winced and said, "That's what he said: 'him' not 'them'." She said she had felt kind of empty for a long time after that. Like a hen. Like he was a fighting cock and she was a hen in his way . . .

Denise gave me my bar and I fumbled for my wallet. I had a queasy feeling in my stomach. I felt doubly guilty because at the time Dahlia had told me all this I hadn't believed her. Now I had a mental picture of her walking near the edge of an unseen cliff on a pitch black night, carrying a small lighted candle that was flickering in the wind.

Either she was telling the truth or she had a vivid imagination. I felt I was nuts to believe her story, but it got me thinking: Lots of money was tied up in cock fights.

My only experience in the matter was in Calabasis, when a stray cock chased my gray wolf down the block. Even from a distance, the speed and determination of the bird told me that this was one serious piece of poultry.

I also recalled that Vito, a Chicano high-staller, had once explained how much money was bet at a cock fight he'd attended in Oregon a few years back. His wide eyes had popped out as he repeated, "Millions and millions and millions . . ."

Well, it's all an exaggeration, but that was the sum of my experience, except for a mean rooster I once owned that had killed a raccoon. True story, that one. Damn bird tried to mate with my leg on occasion; I'll carry the scars from his talons till the day I die. That's what killed the raccoon: the poisons he carried on his talons from walking around the chicken house all day. He punctured the coon's back, and the coon was too stupid to jump in the Sound's cleansing saltwater, so the wounds festered and he died.

A tingling sensation crept up my scarred leg and I did a little Hitler jig. Ted always corrects me when I call my nerve twitch a Hitler jig. He claims Hitler never jigged like that.

"Couldn't have," he says, "'cause he had no sense of rhythm."

Denise started helping another customer, so I pulled the maple bar out of its bag just a bit and took a huge bite out of it.

Pure heaven.

As I munched I speculated that, just maybe, Dahlia was telling the truth after all; maybe she was over twenty-five.

At this thought, a burst of warm relief spread over me. Since she had entered my life my balls had been manufacturing on overtime.

"Yes! Yes!" I burst out.

My musings were broken by Denise's laughter. She rang up the price of my bar and said, "What you yes'n about? Just look at you. How'd you lose so many pounds? How'd you do it?"

Denise always said that. But this time I snickered. I actually had lost twenty pounds, but I wasn't going to tell her how I did it. I paid my buck-seventy-five check with a two-dollar bill, and with a wink told her to keep the change.

I looked down the maze of arcades and decided that the best place for an overview was right where I was headed—the Goodwin Library. The Market Association meeting was being held there.

I moved on, humming, "She was only sixteen, only sixteen."

Chapter 5

A Typical Public Market Meeting

"A white sport coat, and a pink carnation . . ."

THE MEETING WAS IN the Goodwin Library, upstairs in the old Economy Market Building. At the turn of the century the structure had served as the Market's horse stables. To enter you have to duck under a huge plastic tooth that advertises the resident dentist, then climb the rickety wood stairs up to the library.

Like the Market, the library is historical. The wood-paneled room originally served as the offices of Arthur Goodwin, nephew of Market founder Frank Goodwin. Arthur ran the Market after Frank retired. Frank's office had been deep below the Market, but Arthur built his on the second floor, with huge windows so he could observe the daily activity of the tens of thousands of folks who shopped the stalls each day.

It's said that Authur's ghost can be seen and felt along the hallways and in his office. I can believe it because of the way the old floor creaks. Besides, I think my loose synapses allow me to ride spirits, just like those Ghost Riders in the Sky.

"Yippee-yi-oh!"

Focus!

I give tours of the Market as part of my responsibilities, so I knew Arthur had been a Shakespearean actor cum showman. He had created all the intricate lighting and wood pillars that make the Market look like the set of an old Valentino–Theda Bara desert film.

Thank God for Arthur, because we would never have had this wonderful place without him. His stoic uncle had preferred a more purposeful approach to management. Today, since the Market is publicly owned, Arthur's office is used for public meetings, like this one for the community's Market Association.

As I entered the room I wondered how the Goodwins would have liked the Market's present movers and shakers. Frank would have gagged, but I'm sure Arthur would be proud and charmed at all the colorful critters. Like the wild-eyed and ponytailed Garfield, the Market Association's present leader.

Garfield's board consists of ten members, all like him: not a tie or shirt among them, but with keen eyes and sharp tongues and a profound love for this old place. Trouble is, everybody is coming from different directions, politically. And they're all looking for conspiracies. No wonder: management at the Market has deteriorated since the days of the Goodwins.

The Market was meant for average folks, hard workers, folks who want to control their own destiny, people who don't fit in elsewhere, artists and performers starting out in their careers, individuals dedicated to their own way of life. Management is constantly trying to create artificial rules that choke this rapids-filled river of Life Force. But artificial rules don't work; the Market moves too swiftly. There's no time for rules, just guidelines and on-the-spot decisions. Bad management is the chief reason I became "Fishmonger Emeritus."

I was preparing myself mentally because everyone overreacts at meetings like this. But when I walked in and surveyed all the empty seats, I relaxed.

Thank the stars, I thought, only three board members. They may look fired up, but they can't do too much damage: no quorum.

I sat down on one of the folding chairs toward the rear of the room and tried to focus on the subject of the moment. Management had proposed a parking validation plan that Garfield didn't like. Personally, I thought it was a good plan, but Garfield was pushing for an alternative rather than adopting and building on the proposed one. This is always the problem, as I see it, when management loses credibility: anything they try to do becomes suspect.

It was going to be a long meeting. When management has no credibility, any rule or proposal is going to be ignored. In fact, they typically inspire opposition. Why can't those who say they want to operate the Market efficiently understand this?

Realizing that my mind had begun wandering into the dangerous world of management clichés, I naturally pulled out my pipe and lapsed into a thinking posture. From the head of the table, Garfield immediately flayed into me about the dangers of smoking, and the three board members nodded in agreement.

Gothic America in the politically correct Nineties!

I tried to explain that I wasn't going to smoke, just pose a little with the pipe—you know, like Hugh Hefner—but it didn't matter to them. They explained that I was looking like I was. A motion was made and passed stating that I had to put my pipe away. I thought about pointing out that the motion was illegal because there was no quorum, but I simply shrugged, put the pipe back in its pouch, zipped it up and nursed my hurt feelings.

I glanced out the wall of windows. The huge clock showed it was nearing noon. I noticed that the Lamborghini had parked. I suddenly remembered that, in my haste to leave Bugsy's, I had forgotten to shut down my office.

Damn! Focus!

As I rose to leave I saw that the driver of the Lamborghinni—Ricci—was exiting his car. At least I presumed it was Ricci.

Yes, it was Ricci.

He had parked his car next to the box crusher where Dahlia had landed three days before. The Aerostar driver had also found a spot, a bit further up, just under the eaves holding the big pots of geraniums, right where the north arcade section of the Market begins.

Three dark-suited men purposefully got out of the van and made a beeline for Ricci. All three wore black hats with stingy brims, just like in the movies. Ricci wore a light gray tailor-made suit.

Hmm, Ricci and his brothers? Where's Mama and Papa?

No, there were no parents present. These were hoods. Heavyweight hoods.

The heavies stood around the box crusher platform like they were holding a conference. A double irony was that it looked as though the tall driver of the Aerostar was actually in charge rather than Ricci.

I glanced back at the board members: Barbara, long-haired leather worker straight from the sixties; Jennifer, grocery store owner in bib overalls and apron; Art the deli operator, covered with flour from rolling out dough for his famous fresh-baked sandwich rolls, huge gut busting out of a faded T-shirt advertising the Kansas City Zoo. And of course Garfield. Garfield in his madras plaid shorts and Supersonics jersey with Gus Williams' number on it. To give you an idea how old the jersey was, Gus played for the Sonics in the early Eighties. Red white and blue suspenders holding up his shorts completed Garfield's outfit.

I looked down under the table at three pairs of dirty Nikes shuffling and shifting as they matched their owners' intense emoting. No socks. I hoped the ghost of Arthur Goodwin was watching the drama.

I returned my attention to the scene unfolding outside, figuring that the conservatively dressed slicks down below probably had a more direct goal in mind. Finding Dahlia?

Ricci had apparently passed out pieces of paper—photographs?—to each of his goons. Oddly, one of the goons was laughing as he examined his. Even weirder, Ricci and the taller dude weren't laughing at all. Then the four of them fanned out into the Market in different directions.

If my theory was correct, what Ricci had passed out were pictures of Dahlia, so why were the goons laughing?

I didn't understand it.

Actually, it was refreshing to see so much decisiveness going on at the box crusher, because in the library the arguments were becoming downright emotional.

Disturbing questions raced through my mind: Dahlia is safe, isn't she? Of course she is; she's on the *Exacto* in Eagle Harbor. Isn't she?

I weighed the pros and cons of the goons' discovering this fact. My affair with her was the talk of the Market, but Market folks don't tell strangers about Market business.

As usual when I get nervous, I reached for my food—in this case the maple bar—and began chewing on it like a cud. The board paid me no notice. For the most part they accepted me as some sort of necessary nuisance they had to tolerate.

I brushed crumbs off my legal pad and realized I hadn't bothered to take notes. Usually it would be full.

Focus!

I drummed my fingers and decided to return to Bugsy's.

I had no sooner excused myself than I became the focal point of one of Garfield's diatribes about my being some sort of spy for management.

"What's the matter, Deacon? Can't take the heat?" he challenged, looking at his board members to gauge the effect of his quip. "It's your pipe, isn't it. Got to suck on it?" He chugged from his coffee cup. "Got a tobacco addiction, eh?"

I didn't answer, but bowed graciously and left.

As I retraced my steps, I recalled that I had warned Dahlia not to leave the tug or use the phone. I didn't want her messing with her recent past. That included looking for the street musicians and, especially, not trying to contact Ricci. I figured only time would heal her wounds. And time was on her side if only she could learn to slow down.

I smirked, then grimaced. I didn't want her to go; I wanted her. She brought so much to my life.

I should call her, I thought. But then, what would I tell her? That Ricci and three goons were hunting her?

It seemed to me that Dahlia had a moth-to-flame fixation on the guy, even though she kept getting burned. When we had talked about him she had become animated in a cheesecake sort of way, which had told me that she thought she was well experienced.

Well, mature in things she actually wasn't.

But, hell, it was confusing. Like her age. One minute she seemed so young; the next she displayed an experience level far beyond what most women understand at any age.

I mean, she actually loves me, I thought. Big, fat, old me. I've been used many times by women, but never loved.

She must have had hyperactive older brothers. It wasn't like she was a whore. No way. Like Marilyn Monroe, she needed love and plenty of it. I never realized how much love I needed, either.

It made us a perfect pair.

I had a flash that maybe I should read Joe Dimaggio's life story.

I shook myself in anger. No flippancy, buddy boy!

I was convinced that she was relatively safe on the *Exacto*. To find her, Ricci would have to link her to me—Who would tell him?—then find out where I lived.

Then what?

Then he would have to figure out the ferry system and find Eagle Harbor. Then find the *Exacto* in a three-mile-long harbor. Then he'd have to row out to the tug, so he would have to find a rowboat!

Then . . . then. . . .

No, I felt she was quite safe.

I halted at the landing at Post Alley and surveyed the view across the main arcade. At the end of Kim's vegetable stall, framed by row upon row of his brightly colored vegetables, sat Rachel, with her frozen impish grin. I slowly walked toward her with the realization that Dahlia might not have stayed aboard. What if she had left the island and returned to the city? I had taken the dinghy, but I had also pointed out the inflated raft tied at the side of the tug in case she needed something from the store.

Damn! I'm stupid, I thought.

I stopped at Rachel's side, wondering what would prompt Dahlia to leave? Boredom? That's what would do it.

I started down to my scooter when I heard an aid car's siren coming closer. The car turned into Pike Place, shoving bike, pedestrian and cars to the side of the street.

I found myself walking after it, going north across the main arcade, right toward the spot where I'd seen the goons park their cars. I didn't even stop to ask if the sharp-looking fishmongeress would be on duty. Like Dahlia I felt compelled, a moth to a hot light.

Straight over the gangplank to a waiting green shark with its snout wide open. . . .

It was still early, so it was easy to maneuver through the customers crowded around the vegetable stalls. Where the aid car had stopped, a crowd was hovering over a red-faced tourist. He was sitting on the sidewalk in an undignified heap, one too many cameras strung around his neck. The medics were trying to untangle the straps so they could open the poor guy's shirt.

I could tell by his face that he was hurting. As I passed by, I thought about my table at Bugsy's and hesitated. I had to close up my office. That was supposed to be my focus priority. If I didn't make it back I could always buy a pizza.

What the hell was I doing chasing New Yorkers? I didn't have to know who these guys were. I already knew, dammit. They were just tourists. Canasta partners on vacation. Mahjong sales reps in town for a convention. Gamblers ready to wager on a hydroplane race. Not mobsters. Not in Seattle.

I laughed to myself in a giddy way. I was really frightened. Why the fuck was I doing this? Just head home, I told myself.

I tried to retreat but it was too late. I had become fixated— Moth to a light. I spied two goons across the street and another heading down into the north arcade. They all had dark suntans under their stingy brims.

It seemed so funny. They were so obvious in their dark suits. The one that headed down the arcade craft area was causing quite a stir. The craftspeople were pitching their wares at him in earnest. Evidently, they'd mistaken him for some visiting executive doing some last-minute shopping before his plane left from Sea-Tac. Usually when a type like him shows up it means good sales.

That was it. They were doing some last-minute shopping. Those weren't pictures of Dahlia, they were shopping lists!

A helpful craftsperson tried to look at his list, but the goon refused to show it to her. Strange, I thought. The other goons split up. One moved across the street to the Post Alley Market and the other went down the stairs to the lower levels. I didn't see Ricci—or, more accurately, the man I thought was Ricci—so I edged over to his car.

The Lamborghini was equipped with dark, Hollywood glass so it was difficult to make out what was inside. I could see the outline of a small valise and what appeared to be a binocular case on top of a partially opened map. Beside them was a dog-eared paperback. I bent down and peered in.

The map was not of Seattle, as I had assumed, but of Montana, with a bunch of red dots marked on it. There were several maps in a stack, wrapped with a rubber band. The book was a tour book of the Market.

So, Dahlia's story wasn't half-baked after all. I felt a twinge of guilt for not believing her.

I stooped and checked the tires. They were well used. The last thing I did was take down the license plate number.

It read N-172-G, New York State.

Chapter 6

Close Encounter

"All because she's pretty, all because she's so fine . . ."

QUICKLY, I MOVED across the street to a deli that's situated on the sharp tip of a tight, wedge-shaped brick building. This vantage point provided ample viewing of the car and the south end of Pike Place. I was convinced that this was the area Ricci would be coming from. My thoughts narrowed to a tighter focus as I pondered why Ricci would need three goons to help him locate Dahlia.

Does he want to continue his relationship with her? I wondered. It was a funny way to impress her.

My chest tightened at my next thought: Do they want to get rid of a witness? Namely, my little Dahlia?

She had me totally confused about what had transpired between her and Ricci. The first day we spent together she had been in so much fear and pain that she just jabbered away. I hadn't paid much attention to what she said because it sounded far-fetched. The next day she relaxed some and, with that, her stories became more selective in their detail. Yesterday, she was playing coy to the hilt.

I settled in at a table on Post Alley. Normally, it's a most relaxing place, with its grape arbor, but I was disrupted when I turned to look to the north and saw one of the stingy-brims working his way down the street.

I gulped and expelled some gas—farted, dammit!—because he looked as though he were coming straight towards me. Instead, he veered into the popular alley coffee bar. It was fifty-fifty that if he walked through the place he would end up in another part of the Market and miss me. So I relaxed a bit.

I glanced toward the south, thinking I would see Ricci. I didn't, but I did see Garfield through the Goodwin Library window. He was now standing on top of a table, trying to make a point. From my perch, it looked as though he was putting on quite a performance. I wished I were back in the safety of the library, being entertained by him rather than feeling like live bait, to be used for snaring Dahlia.

I started nervously doing the handjive, slapping my elbows, then my thighs. I hadn't done that since I was fifteen.

"Bo Diddely, Bo Diddely, buy me a diamond ring," I sang, out of tune.

I looked across the street again, at Ricci's green machine. Two Market garbage men in green uniforms were breaking down a load of cardboard boxes and stuffing them into the mouth of the nearby crusher. Their uniforms were the same color as Ricci's car.

Out-of-town visitors gazed at them with bemused looks that, to me, read: "My God, is that a Seattle-style garbage truck?" One couple took a photo of the garbage guys posing in front of the car.

The hair at the nape of my neck bristled as I registered the presence of a stingy-brimmed goon coming back out of the coffee bar. I turned, and sure enough, he was headed down Post Alley straight toward me. I scolded myself for looking like a trapped rabbit. My mind screamed at me to do something—anything—so as not to be so obvious!

I opened my attaché case, pulled out the stack of mail I'd picked up at Bugsy's and quickly tore open the first envelope in the stack. Out of the corner of my eye I saw the goon advancing.

I began to smell my own sweat.

Damn!

I examined the letter, reading every word, mouthing each syllable slowly. It was an announcement for another Market meeting—to be held the next day—of the Design and Review Committee. On the agenda was a list of businesses that wanted to set up in the Market. There were four of them: a flower arranger, a shoe repairman, a fried chicken outlet and a ceramist. I knew that the odds were heavily against any of these four making it, because of all the lobbying the established Market businesses would be doing. The committee would be meeting to prepare for Wednesday's four o'clock meeting of the Historic Commission. It was yet another meeting I hadn't planned to attend because, because . . .

A thought reared up in my head: Because I was going to take Dahlia and cruise around San Juan Island!

The *Exacto*! That's what we'd do.

My concentration made my worrywarts recede. I looked around. Damn the worrywarts! The goon had simply walked by without even a glance. I cleared my nose with a snigger. When I had collected myself, I looked up . . . directly into the face of Ricci, who was towering over his car.

His searching intensity made me feel, just for an instant, that he had singled me out, but he then turned and looked just as intently down Pike Place. He reached over and grabbed a piece of paper from his windshield. It looked like a parking ticket. Did he look nervous, or was I imagining it?

As he got into his machine and sat there studying the slip of paper, I took a deep breath and regained some cool. I turned and saw my reflection in a dirty window alongside the deli. I looked as though I'd been dragged through a field of pain by my earlobes.

I turned back to watch Ricci's car. The narrow Hollywood windows prevented me from seeing what he was doing, but after a bit he rolled down the side window and tossed out a balled-up piece of paper. The wad hit the brown, crumpled wreck of a Ford parked next to him. I was pretty sure he'd pitched the parking ticket since I noticed he had parked in a truck loading zone. Then he opened the door, reached down, and retrieved the piece of paper.

He was playing it safe.

Ricci started the machine and revved the powerful engine twice, attracting the attention of a pack of tourists holding bunches of brightly colored helium balloons. The group hovered around the machine as it slowly backed out. It seemed like there were a hundred balloons floating above the car.

Well, maybe eighty.

Shit! Okay, twenty.

Bullshit.

"Bullshit," I muttered out loud, drumming my fingers nervously, trying to keep from sinking into a funk.

I was angry at all the attention the creep was getting. I saw how crowded Pike Place was and realized it would take him at least twenty minutes to move down the street, so I felt a little better.

My synapses began flickering. I felt uncomfortable. Something was itching at the back of my brain.

Focus!

I turned and scanned the little plaza. Across from me were three tables, occupied by diners eating early lunches. Above me, the old bricks of the building that housed the deli were absorbing the sun's light and heat. The play of light seemed to make every single brick unique.

I zeroed in on one brick. Its deep redness drew me invitingly into its mass. My cheek brushed its solid raspy surface. Inward I moved. The surface had little craters like the moon. I sensed pockmarks with the edges of my mind. Deeper I went into my rectangular moon. In a crevice sat Dahlia, smiling at me. She was holding a ladybug.

I was brought out of my escape hatch by a flap of a wing. I

blinked and saw several pigeons sitting in a row high up on the roof line. One lone seagull perched at the end of the file.

I studied the gull. It wasn't Israel. I tried to relocate my brick among the thousands in the wall, but the opportunity had passed.

Focus!

I looked over, watched Zelmondo make a grease-dripping gyro and realized what had been munching on the back of my mind: It was time to forage again. The next order of business was ordering a gyro. Besides, I reasoned, gyros are so filling eating one would settle my nerves.

As Zelmondo unfolded the pocket bread I thought how much he looked like Ricci. Except for the eyes. Also, Zelmondo had the demeanor of a gentleman while Ricci's movements gave the impression of a loose laser looking for something to slice.

I laughed and thought: In Santa Barbara, Ricci wouldn't stand out at all. When I go there to visit old friends I stand out like a classic big movie star. I've got true girth. On the beach all the girls come up to me and give me leering looks right in front of their boyfriends. Randy old me leers right back.

I had begun dreaming of the tanned blonde ladies of the beach when Zelmondo yelled "Wake up!" and handed me my gyro wrapped in a bag. My recollection of my beach days had me unconsciously flexing my arms and shoulder muscles. Zelmondo began flexing back in mock competition.

No contest. The tattoo around his biceps, which read "U.S. Navy, give 'em hell!" stretched a full three inches when he flexed. There were no tattoos to show off under the sleeve of my sweatshirt.

As I paid, I noticed that Ricci's car had barely moved because a truck was offloading in the street. One of the goons had returned and stopped to talk with Ricci.

Suddenly I got an idea. I turned to rush up Post Alley, leaving Zelmondo doing a solo. My route—a shortcut through a passage where Doc Shogun has his naturopathic practice—took me to the Aerostar in seconds.

The first thing I noticed was the chalk mark on the rear tire, placed by a meter maid about a half-hour earlier, probably at the same time she ticketed Ricci's car. I looked down the street and saw Hilde, the stern meter maid, working her way slowly back to the van. It's hourly parking along Pike Place and she probably had her route timed to the minute. What a way for the city to have to make a buck. Through the line of parked cars I saw that Ricci and the goon were still talking, so I jotted down the license plate number of the van and took a deep gander in the window. Again, heavily tinted glass impeded my view.

The van appeared to be well lived in. The floorboards were cluttered with bottles and newspapers. There was a stack of impressive-looking papers clipped together on the back seat. I could make out the company heading on the top page of the stack. It read: "Chicken Jive Inn." I scratched my head. Weird name for a hen house, I thought.

I turned and leaned my back on the van, thinking. It seemed odd, a name like that. Maybe it just had a familiar ring to it. As I opened the brown bag and removed my sandwich, one of the stingy-brimmed goons—the driver—jammed his hawklike head straight down into my face. My gyro dropped before I could take a bite.

"What you doing, Jake?" he demanded in massive Brooklynese.

I stood bolt upright in fear, which is hard for me to do, what with my stoop and all, and emitted a high, choking laugh.

"I was looking for the owner," I blurted. "If this is your car, I would advise you to wipe out the chalk marks that the meter maid put on your tire so you won't get a ticket."

I looked down the street and pointed at Hilde. Behind her, Ricci and the other goon were still in animated conversation. I started sweating, and again felt he was going to smell fear. I was one big, trapped rabbit.

The goon nosed deep into my face, garlic breath so strong I almost choked from holding my breath until it dawned on me that he couldn't smell a thing with his overpowering foul mouth. I relaxed, forcing myself to ignore the odor.

"And why would you want to do a favor for the occupants of this car," he demanded.

"Sir, this is Seattle," I said, letting out a deep breath. "I noticed you're from out of state and I didn't want you to get a ticket."

That got him thinking real good, and he laughed.

"Yeah! It's funny. When I got this here latte up at that donut shop, the girl came running after me just to make sure I got my lousy twenty cents change. Boy, that bitch was really taking a chance. In Manhattan, if she left like that, her joint would be stripped in seconds."

My eyes wandered to the meter maid behind him. Finally, he moved back and turned to see what I was looking at. When he saw her, he went behind the Aerostar, bent down and wiped off the chalk marks.

"Hey, thanks, buddy," he yelled back at me as I made my exit, breathing a deep sigh of relief.

As I walked away I looked back and saw that the rats that lived in the storm drain had already squeezed most of my gyro through the grate. I shrugged my rounded shoulders and muttered to myself.

"He's going to pay for that. NOBODY messes with my gyro."

Chapter 7

Georgio Solano

"Oh solo mio . . ."

I GOT OUT OF THERE none too soon. At the first vegetable stall I stopped and watched the Lamborghini as it slowly inched out into Pike Place. A goon was walking alongside the green sportscar, talking with Ricci in the driver's seat.

It was a hell of a note. I wished I could just go up and tell Ricci, if it *was* him, to leave Dahlia alone. Maybe I should challenge him to a duel, I thought. A fight. A fight for her honor. May the best man win and all that.

But these guys didn't look like the fighting type, just the killing type. The confrontation at the Aerostar was a close shave, but the goon wouldn't read anything into it.

I took another deep breath when I realized then and there that these East Coasters wouldn't get any information out of Market people. Dahlia would be safe as long as she stayed aboard the *Exacto*.

As I pushed through the swelling crowds, I heard another siren in the distance. I heard them so many times a day I paid it no mind. They were probably coming to pick up a downed drunk lying comatose in a gutter somewhere. The city is full of gutters. Gutters and drunks. I noticed that the aid car had left with the camera-strapped tourist. Perhaps that was the siren I was hearing. Who keeps count of sirens anymore in this big massive city.

I made my way through the main arcade, purposely avoiding eye contact with Rachel. As I passed her, I did give her a gentle pat that sent a small current of electricity to Paul. But I had things in hand and was able to make my way to the narrow stairway to Post Alley South. It was impossible to pass at the top because a trio of street musicians were sitting there, playing harmonicas as though possessed, and a crowd had gathered around them.

I stopped to listen and decided it was the best version of *"That's all right, Mama"* I had ever heard. One of the guys wore heavy boots and kept the beat by stomping.

I had to get down to my office, so I bypassed them by going up to the "Tongue," but got stuck in another crowd that had gathered around the Speaker's Corner, a section of the market set aside for people with causes. Tall, gaunt Flamingo Red was screaming about the rights of the enslaved factory workers.

Man, was he out of sync—plus sixty, bald, and wearing a ponytail made from his receding sideburns. I didn't think Seattle had any sweatshops left. Or blue collar jobs, for that matter.

I eased around the crowd and was about to proceed down into the tunnel when I stopped and checked Ricci's progress down Pike Place. He had pulled in next to the Aerostar and the three of them were looking around. I reasoned that they were waiting for the fourth goon. Hilde had moved on beyond them and I hit myself for doing them the favor. I thought that the best thing for me to do was go home and be by Dahlia's side until these goons hit the road.

As I hurried down to Bugsy's I thought that I could rig up a lookout system using Market people. They could phone me when the goons were gone.

I ducked into Bugsy's and took a deep breath. First order of business was to make sure Dahlia was safe. As I passed the reception desk I unconsciously reached for the phone, but I hesitated, then put the phone back because I didn't want to alarm her.

I apologized to Antonio for not closing down my office for lunch. He just laughed and said that the joint had only been half full at noon, but that several of the patrons had wondered about the celebrity who was eating behind the screen.

Lea walked by, carrying a couple of tasty-looking beef sandwiches. Since I had lost my gyro, my mouth went all saliva-ish, but I resisted looking her way while I closed shop.

When I finished, I checked my watch and realized I had forty minutes until the next ferry sailed, so I relaxed and ordered a small deep-dish. Lea brought over a glass of TK—Thomas Kemper—a great, great local microbrew. I raised the glass high and saluted.

"To Seattle, the world's greatest gourmandian city."

The brew went down in one slug, so I indulged in another.

I looked out the window and checked my watch again as I watched the *Walla Walla* glide into view. It was my cue to leisurely saunter to Colman Dock, since the ferry would have to unload before reloading the car decks. I figured I had about half an hour.

The pizza arrived, so I tucked a napkin into the neck of my sweatshirt and spread it out wide, making a white diamond over my ample girth, then proceeded to gobble the house specialty in about ten minutes flat. I gave out a long, slow, satisfied burp, finished my beer, locked up the office, paid Lea with a ten dollar bill and bid my hosts adieu.

As I climbed up Post Alley to fetch—damn, I mean get—my scoot, I looked up and stopped dead in my tracks. I could see the snout of the green Lamborghini near the First and Pike stoplight. Ricci got a green light as I hurriedly prepared to depart, but I was delayed because of the old motorcycle helmet, which I had to force on my head.

"Moth to light, moth to light . . ."

I finally got started and sped up onto the sidewalk, turning into the street at the curb's wheelchair dip. In my haste, I cut in front of Porch, who was pushing Prez in his wheelchair. Porch is a recovering alcoholic and as ornery as they come.

"Sorry guys, I'm in a hurry," I yelled out.

"Shove it!" responded Porch.

I felt bad about my rudeness because Prez had lost both his legs to diabetes, and Porch, helping people like he does, had really turned into something of a grumpy saint.

I continued out into the street as the light changed, just glimpsing Ricci two blocks ahead turning up University Street.

I took off down Pike and quickly made a right down Second, a much quicker street than First. So quick, in fact, that I had to slow to a stop at mid-block to allow Ricci to pass when he had the green light. I followed at a distance until I saw him smartly turn in at the Grand Hotel, Seattle's top of the line.

Ricci had every set of eyes looking at his machine as he exited and handed the keys to the attendant. They exchanged some words that made the attendant smile, and Ricci briskly entered through the hotel's ornate front doors.

I parked the scoot by the newspaper boxes and matched Ricci step for step, getting to the attendant just as he finished placing a numbered tag under the windshield of the Lamborghini. He was just about to get in when I came up.

"Man, what a fantastic car," I said. "Is it yours?" That flattered the weekend NASCAR warrior no end. He rubbed some imaginary dust off the fender, possessively.

"I wish," he replied. "It's Mr. Solano's. A guest of the hotel." He slipped behind the wheel. "A hundred grand gets you two-hundred mph."

He turned the key and revved up the twelve pistons. It sounded like a Wonder Warthog fart.

Well, as I would imagine it, that is. If he could fart.

I mean, I hate flashy cars that cost too much. I thought about my own car, a 1947 Buick Roadmaster. Now, that's a car! I vowed that when I got it restored and running I'd match Ricci, flash to flash! They were the same color, too, except mine was dull from age. Well, dammit, I would rub the color right back up to snuff.

My mindset on the car continued as I returned to my scoot. Old Dutch had given it to me. He had found me walking through his backyard that serves as a graveyard to hundreds of weed-filled cars from the late Forties to the early Sixties. He had inherited them from his pop who had worked as a Bainbridge Island towtruck operator during that era. A 1950 fishbowl Studebaker was my favorite.

The ferry boat's departing blast broke my train of thought.

"Damn, missed another ferry!" I cursed out loud.

A couple walking by heard me. I was a bit embarrassed, so I reached in my pocket for a Snickers bar, but when I did so they scurried on. I stood there watching them, wondering what to do next. I had another hour to burn until the next ferry. I snapped my fingers and slapped my thighs.

"Yes, of course" I said.

Another couple stared at me worriedly as I remounted my scoot and lit out for the public library, which was a few blocks closer to the dock. I was there in a minute and parked alongside a bank of newspaper stands. Vandenberg Billy stood at the entrance and hit me with his raincheck, so I gave him a five-dollar bill. Old Billyvan beamed and bowed and brayed.

I walked across the marble floor lobby, passed through the security turnstile and passed on to the newspaper section that contained a whole shelf of books and clippings devoted to the Syndicate. The librarian there was very helpful, and directed me to another load of information filed under the heading of "The Mafia."

I took an armload of material and found an empty table where

I could spread it out. After a few minutes of sifting through the clippings, I returned to the information desk and asked for a chronology of events relating to the Mafia's various families.

As with many Americans, I have a fascination for the subject and knew many of the famous names, but I'd never come across the name of Solano. I looked through clippings from the big-time centers like New York and Chicago, with no luck. I then researched Miami and what I thought were second-tier organized crime centers. Still nothing.

A soft, faint toot penetrated the library's silence. It registered on my brain that the ferry was arriving and that I should go, but I had a sharp focus now and nothing was going to take me away from it until I found what I was searching for. A file on Philadelphia Mafia activity led me to a sub-file on Pittsburgh, a city not usually associated with the Family. It was here that I struck paydirt.

One Georgio Solano from Sardinia, but of Sicilian blood, came to the U.S. shortly after Lucky Luciano was retired to Sicily. Georgio was a quiet member of the Mafia and only moved into the mainstream after a big bust in 1963 in up-state New York. He was considered an expert in laundering dirty money and blending it with clean by making investments in legitimate businesses.

Then my eye caught a small headline in a *New York Times* article that read, *"Ricci Solano suspected of murdering Miami girlfriend."*

Oh boy! Paydirt! I said to myself. I began to read.

"Georgio Solano, a little-known mobster, died on February 14, 1992. Solano is survived by his wife, Estella, and three sons, Rico, Vido and Ricci."

So his youngest son, Ricci, was born in 1968, I thought. Hmmm, that would make him about twenty-five.

"The Solano Family settled in Yonkers," the article continued, *"where they are considered to be as respectable as anybody. As a teenager, Ricci shocked the community when he beat a fellow student to*

*a bloody pulp. Later, as a college student at NYU, he studied film
making, but was arrested after making pornographic movies starring
himself and some co-eds. Next, he was arrested for rape and for beating a young woman, who was found wandering the streets of Yonkers just a few blocks from Solano's family home. The charges, however, were dropped and Solano has no record.*

*"In 1987, after an apparent exile to Miami, he was arrested as
a suspect in connection with the brutal bludgeoning murder of a
young woman whom he'd dated for a year. Again, no charges were
filed. Solano disappeared from view after that incident. Many people
who know the family feel that the last situation brought on Georgio's
death. The Mafia leaders apparently were greatly displeased with
young Ricci and especially the loss of a most valued lieutenant in
Georgio. Thousands showed up to pay their respects at his funeral."*

I fumbled in my pocket for some change to photocopy the article, and ruminated that another chapter in the Solano saga was
unfolding here in Seattle. A deep pool of acid pain formed in the pit
of my stomach as I wondered how it would end. As I walked to the
photocopy area my thoughts started rambling.

What was I worried about? Dahlia? That she wasn't home? That
she left me for Ricci? Why should that bother me? I was over forty—
well, fifty. What was it about youth? Why was I intimidated by the
situation? What was I trying to do? Possess her? Demand that she
stay with me? Hijack her? Keep her on the *Exacto* against her will?

I was working myself into a confusing funk. I mean, I rarely
had such a high as I shared with her. What the hell was going on in
my mind? Was my macho evolving into a sort of patermaternalitis?
Was I turning into a kind of aging hermaphrodite? Was my sex really a kind of nurturing meal she demanded, as though she were a
child in need? Was this my last tango in Seattle?

Oh shit! Bullshit! Maybe I should start wearing ponytails.

I rubbed my beard. I felt like the world's biggest heel, but that was swiftly followed by a surge of self-righteous anger that involuntarily squared my shoulders.

I took a deep breath and coughed slightly as I cleared my throat. I walked over to the long, well-worn wooden counter with its tall piles of magazines waiting to be re-filed. I placed my stuff down and waited for the library clerk's attention so I could pay for my photocopies.

The clerk reminded me of someone. She had about her what we called in Hollywood "a typifying statement": tall, slightly dumpy, but with a tinge of spunk deep in her eyes. Her graying hair was balled so severely that the skin of her face was stretched taut. I fantasized about her private life:

Hmmm. . . she has five kids, most likely; one died very young; her old man works at Boeing and drinks three quarts of Bud after work; she lives in the north-end suburbs and has to sub at the library to make the house payments . . .

"Say, haven't I seen you on the Walla Walla?" she asked, derailing my thought train.

Yup, that was where I saw her. I nodded, getting red in the face.

"I only see you once in awhile," she continued, "because I usually fly my floatplane to work. But I have a photographic memory."

My blush spread all over my face.

"It's quite a coincidence, meeting you here," she continued. "I only volunteer for the library when I'm not taking film crews to location sites around the Sound. That will be one-oh-eight including tax."

I gave her a five.

"Say, didn't you have your daughter with you a few days ago," she asked. "Nice looking kid, but you really should get her to eat more." She chuckled mischievously. "But she's not your daughter, right? I know how you feel; my boyfriend is twenty."

She handed me my change, smiling, showing big even teeth.

"Good luck, Sweet Tooth," she said.

I stumbled out of the library, red as a baboon's rump.

What is this world coming to?

On the way out, I hesitated next to the phone booth and gathered my composure. I stole a look back at the librarian. She smiled and waved; I waved back. I needed that.

I turned back to the phone, picked up the receiver then put it back. I reached into my pocket for a quarter but just jangled my change and walked away. I was holding onto the conviction that Dahlia was safe on the boat and that I shouldn't alarm her.

"I'm a-coming home, baby, baby, wahoo!" I sang.

I checked my watch—time to hurry—straddled my scoot and made a dash for the dock. Only to miss the ferry once again.

"Damn!" I shouted. Several people glanced at me.

I gave the ticket-taker my ticket, parked my scoot on the dock, then went upstairs to the bar adjacent to the waiting room. I ordered a hot latte to warm me up after my brisk run down from the library. I spied two snappy looking pronto pups and ordered them along with my brew. The clerk didn't understand what I meant by pronto pups, so I pointed to them. I explained that I wasn't about to call them corndogs "because it makes them sound as though they're made of corn, not meat."

"Say what?" she said, a look of confusion on her dull face.

"I like red meat, real red meat!" I announced.

"So do I," she confided, blushing a bit and hunching her shoulders, coy like, as she prepared my latte. It was ready in a flash because she used one of those new-fangled machines that cranks out lattes, espressos and all sorts of Italian-sounding coffee beverages in a flash. It's one modern innovation I approve of.

I thought of Ricci's expensive car, then of Dutch's backyard full of magnificent, rusting machines. There were three Hudson Hornets. When I was in high school, my friend Johnny and I had cruised around in one of his old man's Hudsons. Johnny's dad had owned a distributorship in Carpenteria, so we cruised in a different Hudson every week.

In addition to his Hudsons, Dutch also had a battered Healy that took me back to L.A. in the sixties when I had owned a fantastic 100-6 model. Once, I had picked up a girl at the Raincheck Bar, and we had gone cruising out to Malibu with no top. It was the only way, since the Healy's top was getting repaired.

Inevitably, we got a little passionate. The previous owner had adjusted the front seats so they could be flattened over the back jump seat, and I took advantage of this. For privacy's sake, I also managed to get the tonneau cover zipped over my partner's bare rump as she enthusiastically straddled me. As we got it on, she went a little crazy and split the cover. As we climaxed, for some reason we both looked up . . . straight into the cockpit windshield of a huge ten-ton semi, where a guy, eating a submarine sandwich, sat watching the action. The rat must have crept up on us when he saw the tonneau cover bobbing.

Honest, Mrs. Alice.

After we arranged our dignity we headed for the Moonshadows Restaurant just down the PCH—Pacific Coast Highway. Funny thing happened when we got there: I could have parked right out front next to this 3.8 Jag sedan, but instead chose a side-area parking spot. Just as we parked, a ten-ton semi lost control and plowed into the Jag—right where we would have been parked. I often wondered if it was the submariner getting it off his way.

I thought about that for many years.

God, I had loved that little Healy as if it were my girlfriend. What would a mint one cost today? Thirty grand?

Well, back to old Dutch. He had been in the process of tidying up his backyard because of all the new construction going up around his property. What had once been an area of small houses was now getting filled with fancy ones for seniors.

One day while I was helping him he was in an expansive mood and asked me if I wanted one of his cars. Though I didn't react quickly and point to the Healy, he saw the direction of my gaze—toward the little sports car.

"Sure," he said. "Take the Roadmaster."

The Buick had been parked behind the Healy, which was almost lost in the overgrowth. It was the Buick Dutch thought I was ogling.

The keys were in the door, and Dutch told me that we were in luck because the hardest part of sorting out the yard was finding and then matching the keys to the car.

And that's how I got Henrietta, for that's what I named her.

No regrets. We rolled her down to my parking space at the dock and there she sits. I've told myself twenty times that I'll get to restoring her one of these days. We actually got her fired up two months ago.

When I introduced Dahlia to Henrietta, she positively had to make love in the car that very night, so we got some good red and camped out in the back seat, initiating our affair.

I laughed, for a thought surfaced: Had Ricci ever done it with Dahlia in the Lamborghini? I'd have to ask her once I got back to the boat.

I took out the paper that I'd scribbled my notes on, stared at the license plate numbers and thought of Rollo.

Rollo is the fluttery garbage man at the Market. I call him my "little brother" because he's my size. He once told me that his brother worked for the State of New York.

Perhaps, just perhaps . . .

Well, I'm sure he wouldn't mind if I asked to have his brother check the plates.

I still had half an hour until the next ferry left, so I returned to my scoot, checked out at the ticket office, and returned to the Market to hunt for Rollo. He's never hard to find because he's so big and in uniform. When I tracked him down, he was most helpful, and said he would use the management's fax to send my requests to his brother immediately. I was about to leave when I spotted Ernesto, a security guard who'd told me about cockfights.

Damn, I had vowed I was going to make the next ferry, but the security guards work odd hours, and this was my only chance. Ernesto was most helpful in telling me about the betting and the number of people who attended the fights. He said it was a very big business, and that fights were usually held close to chicken farms late in the evening. He said a big problem was that the law was always trying to break them up.

I asked him how many he'd attended.

He said many in Washington and Oregon, and a couple of times he had gone to Montana and Idaho to watch a few fights. He said he'd owned several fighting cocks himself. One was a four-time winner that made him enough money to buy his house. He told me that the cocks fight to the death. One survivor.

He closed the conversation by asking me if he could buy my crazy rooster. The rooster had chased Hussy, a big, fat neighbor girl off the property when I lived on a farm in the center of the island. Chasing Hussy was no mean feat. The girl was as ornery as the rooster was horny. My leg involuntarily twitched.

My thoughts wandered as usual, and I wondered how Hussy was doing. She had a proprietary crush on me. I found out that word about my extended "date" had gotten to her at the bar she tended on the island when I went to buy a sixpack.

"With a pencil-neck!" as she put it, accusingly.

I smirked at that one, but had to duck quick to avoid her purposeful roundhouse swing at my head. She was powerful: five feet two, three hundred pounds, and not an ounce of fat on her.

The toot of the arriving ferry got me scrambling to my scoot. I'd paid in advance so I would be able to just breeze through and onto the car deck. With a sigh of relief I wedged the helmet on and buzzed down out of the market.

At the waterfront a young lass on her bike appeared going the opposite direction. She was wearing some very short shorts, with her pink undies peeping out. The seat she was perched on had a white overlay. Her butt was way up in the air. She knew exactly what she was doing.

Pump, *pump, PUMP.*

It reminded me of my old Paul being worked over.

I knew I had at least twenty minutes, so I veered right, rather than left, to follow her. I had no choice, for my nose had inflamed and was leading me like a duck to water. In moments like these I cursed Mrs. Alice, for it was she who had set me on my randy road. It was because of her I had no choice but to follow the bike girl—none.

"Focus" I shouted frantically, realizing I had to return to the ferry. The girl turned and gave me the finger.

Now, now, Mrs. Alice . . .

With that, I slowed to turn back to get the ferry. I caused a mild traffic jam because I'd gotten in the path of about thirty male bicyclists, two bull-dyke motorcyclists, and a lone driver of a bouncing pickup truck, all straining forward as if being pulled by the same invisible string.

After I made an illegal U-turn, a cop at the curb pulled me over and cited me. I told him I had to get overseas, and couldn't he just give me a break? He was merciless, though, and went over to his car and radioed for a make on me. I told him it was all the fault of that girl on the bike for pedaling in such a skimpy outfit.

He stared at me as if I was some sort of out-of-control pervert. Finally, he got his information and cited me for both an illegal U-turn and for not having my helmet strapped on.

Nice guy.

I heard the toot of the departing ferry. I started the scoot and put my helmet on, cinching it nice and legal like. I turned to see if it was clear, and there was the girl, again peddling back toward us. I watched the stone-faced cop lick the end of his pencil.

Seattle. Setup city. Hmmm.

Now I was in a real quandary as I putted around potholes to the terminal. I had missed the ferry. What was I to do? I saw four phone booths in a row and stopped, dialed and waited. The phone rang and rang, but no one answered. After the sixth ring, the answering machine clicked on and I heard the tune I'd put on yesterday morning at Dahlia's urging. It was "I'm a Yankee Doodle Dandy." After a riff I heard my own voice.

"Your nickel. Shoot."

Proudly I hung up without leaving a message. Then I stood there for a full minute, gulped, lost my cool, and redialed. This time, at the end of the message I wasn't so proud.

"Baby, I'll be home on the next ferry," I cooed. "I love you, Baby Snookums."

I blew her a kiss and replaced the receiver.

Chapter 8

Askew at Arms

"Mr Postman can't you see, is there a letter, a letter for me?
Please, Mr. Postman . . ."

A S I STOOD THERE, staring at the four phones, I had a weird urge to try another phone. Maybe a different one would get through. The afternoon air was clean because a light, crisp breeze was blowing. Several seagulls were converging on a roadkill that had been dumped in the bed of the trolley track that runs along the edge of the roadway. I surmised that they had about five minutes to dine until the next trolley came by.

I muttered, "What to do? What to do? What to do?"

Check the situation, Deacon, check it off. Focus.

But I'd never had a situation like this! Frantically, I wracked my brain:

Ted, my man of logic! But he was in his cabin on Mt. Rainier.

Timber Dan, my palm reader! But he wasn't in the Market until Friday.

Damn! Sussing this out was a job for Ted.

No phone, no phone . . .

Hercules, I snapped! Herc! My savior!

I stared at my island across the bay.

Is Dahlia at the store? I wondered.

No, she didn't have any money. But she knew where my "passenger only" ferry tickets were.

Holy shit!

She's here, I realized. She's in Seattle. She must be. I knew it.

I felt a cold sweat form on my chest as the guilt took over my consciousness. Then I started losing it. I gasped for breath.

I didn't warn her. I had thought I shouldn't warn her, that it would upset her.

She needed me. Oh God, she needed me.

Foc–foc–focus!

What the fuck to do.

Go to Herc; get a read; find some balance.

I cleared my throat and settled down. Swearing sobered me up. I pride myself on rarely swearing, but this time it was necessary.

Bullshit.

I scooted back out, asked for another pass from the grunting ticket taker, then rode back up to the Market. On the way I recalled how I had met Hercules.

It had been thirty years before, when he was an extra in Hollywood. Back then he was a pleasant sort. He had come from the Belgian Congo. Now the country is called "Zaire." He was a hit with everyone he met because he wasn't uptight. I relaxed as I recalled how it had been.

We had both been taking acting lessons in North Hollywood from James Cain. Herc was wooden, but boy what a presence. Six-foot-eight and moved like a limbo dancer. He could have been a star. Unfortunately, it had been the mid-Sixties and some mean old dope was being manufactured in Venice: LSD hybrids.

One time Herc found himself fallen among predatory company down at the Hinano Bar. He was with two gone-to-seed basketball players as tall as he was, they bought some of this new-fangled dope from a beer bum under the pier, and all three of them lost their minds. One died shortly after the experience; another is still in a looney bin in Kentucky.

Herc never really came down, either, but did manage a focus. He fixated on Barbie Dolls in a very big way. He constructed his first Barbie Doll jalaba—a robe made entirely of Barbie Dolls stitched together—then walked the sixteen-mile length of Sunset Boulevard from the train station to the start of Malibu wearing it.

Once, on a pilgrimage to Oregon to visit the designer of the dolls, Herc was arrested as a public nuisance in Kenwood outside Santa Rosa. Normally as gentle as a saint—as long as no one spoke the name "Ken"—he was totally freaked out by the name of the town. The arrest made the papers and he was saved by a faded movie star living in Ojai. She attempted to make a Barbie Doll cult, centered around Herc. Much to his credit, he rejected all this attention and simply walked on up the Coast Highway, eventually making it to Seattle.

And that's where I found him, wandering around the Market. Here he's considered . . . well, odd but normal in a seer-y sort of way. "Seer-y." Now there's a word for you. Herc is a pretty good seer. Not the same level as Timber Dan, but then who is?

I had arranged Herc's business for him, guiding him through the maze of committees. I thought he never appreciated it because now he considers himself a god. He still does a theatrical act that made him an underground favorite in L.A. I've never personally seen it, but I'm told he is hired to perform at all-female parties.

He apparently arrives wearing his jalaba, then sits in a chair and meditates. After a short bit, his cock will swell and rise (Mrs. Alice, I'm warning you), working its way through the Barbie dolls. As his trance deepens, his cock rises further. He never uses his hands, and eventually he climaxes. Hussy says she saw him once, and that he shot his wad a whole eight feet, splattering it all over all the women present. Then quickly his cock would shrivel, and he would quietly get up and leave without a word.

Focus, focus, FOCUS!

Deek, you've gone too far, I thought. Now you're embellishing your bullshit.

As I parked at the Market I started involuntarily singing, "Those were the days my friend, we thought they'd never end, we'd sing and dance . . ." But it had happened. All of it. It would be lying to myself to say it didn't. It all happened. Back then, L.A. had been my randy capital of the universe.

Thinking about Dahlia had unlocked my mind, tightened my loose synapses, and brought my past hurtling before me. I was in love and had entered a new space. It was like dying and being reborn. Alice to Dahlia at the tender age of fifty-two.

Keep a focus, Deek, I thought. You love the young lady, so start protecting your interests. They want to take her away from you.

I locked the bike and quickly walked down to the lower level ramp to Herc's shop. It had a large star painted on it and a sliding panel that read "unoccupied." Above and inside the star was another sign which simply read, "Hercules the Fortune Teller." I opened the door and walked in.

Inside, the room was gloomy and in shadows. I closed the door and slid the sign to "occupied." Herc was sitting on his throne, a bamboo Lord Jim chair I'd bought him at a thrift store when we were setting up his business. Herc had adapted it to meet his concerns by festooning it with miniature furniture: little chairs, tables, refrigerators, end tables. He'd fastened literally hundreds of pieces of dollhouse furniture to the chair for his Barbie Dolls' comfort.

Herc looked magnificent sitting there, tall and straight of back. His ebony skin was taut over his bulging muscles. Only his eyes showed his age: they were starting to look sunken.

I remembered the one cardinal rule: Don't mention the name "Ken." It drives him berserk. The first time he warns you. The second time he *really* warns you by ripping a Barbie off his chest and chewing off its head. As for the third time, well . . .

Rumor has it that in L.A. Herc once killed a politically correct neurotic who admonished him about his Barbie worship; his body was never found. That was a distinct aberration from Herc's normal demeanor; that is, if it really happened.

Deep down Herc is a professional. He was not only honed as I was by Hollywood, he graduated. He learned how to wait. The one thing in life I never learned, till now, was how to wait. I hate waiting. That's why I never went anywhere with my acting career. Why I never went anywhere, for that matter, in anything I ever tried.

Somehow, Herc has always seemed able to rise above impatience. He can sit for days, seemingly in a trance, waiting for a customer. I shrugged my shoulders. I guess that's his secret: he ain't waiting for a customer, he's just sitting.

He raised his head slowly and looked at me unblinkingly. After a moment recognition flickered in his eyes.

"Master Deacon," he said. "Please. Sit down."

I sat.

"Tell me, Deek—it's hard for me to call you Deacon—what is it that disturbs you so? What questions do you have for me?"

"Herc," I said, "my life today is just too confusing."

Herc looked at me, unblinking. "Well?"

I tried to answer but couldn't. After I'd been silent for maybe a minute, Herc took my hands in his own and turned them over, palms up. His fingers wrapped completely around the fleshy mounds below my thumbs. He closed his eyes tightly, muttering something incomprehensible. Eventually, he began speaking in a sonorous voice.

"A little bug appears at the base of a tall tree in the dead of winter. The bug starts climbing the tree. It seems like an impossible task, and one with no meaning, for the life of the tree is dormant. Each day, the bug climbs upward. Each weekend it rests a bit before relentlessly climbing on. After three months it finally arrives at the top, just as the tree's first tender shoots are beginning to emerge in the warming light of spring."

He stopped talking and just sat there in silence, his eyes closed. I coughed nervously and prepared to leave. Herc still didn't open his eyes.

"Deek," he said deeply, "for you it is five bucks, for other people twenty."

I thanked him and placed a ten spot in the brass urn sitting on a little carved table next to the exit door behind his throne. As I opened the door he yelled at me.

"Deek. Deacon." His tone was reassuring. "Act as you must, but with patience."

I closed the door. A sense of quiet enveloped me, but also a feeling of impending doom.

Chapter 9

Resolve

"Earth angel, earth angel, will you be mine . . ."

HERC HAD ARRANGED his fortune-telling studio as a two-door walk-through so his clients wouldn't have to bump into one another. Wishful thinking. I've rarely seen one customer, much less two at one time.

I went out his exit door, turned right, reentered the third lower level from a little hallway that ran alongside his studio, then crossed its expanse of well-used hardwood floor. As I moved towards the Pine Street stairwell I thought that my subconscious was heeding Herc's advice. I felt much more relaxed, thus much more in charge of the situation.

Unfortunately, it also made me yearn for some carbos.

I opened the heavy wood door to the stairclimb and a brackish Puget Sound breeze swept over me. I hesitated, thinking about returning to the homeyness of the Market's lower levels, but squared my shoulders and continued up to the main arcade.

At the first landing I stopped to gain a bit of breath and sniffed the air again. It smelled distinctly like low tide. My thoughts returned to the ferry: Why the hell did I keep missing it? Was I afraid Dahlia was gone?

Man, I thought, I hate the moment. Give me the past to embellish, the future to dream.

I started walking. What the hell was I philosophizing about? It was simply my chickenshit side causing me to miss the ferries.

I stopped. No, someone was definitely riding my mind. I stood silent for almost a whole minute, searching my synapses, but my mind was a blank. I realized that I was being drawn into a picture; no, into a frame without a picture; no, it had to be a picture.

In a slow monotone, I ad-libbed the blues standard.

"But I'm built for comfort and not for speed; I'm fifty-two years old; I'm Deek. . . .

"Deacon, dammit, Fishmonger Emeritus!"

I reached the main arcade and stood there silently, as though in a trance. I felt myself rising above, removed from my body.

Oh oh. A VERY bad case of loose synapses.

Directly below me I could see Deek watching the fishmongers barking at the customers. They were slick, their banter titillating. Wearing a heavy plastic apron, a young guy I had worked with in my mongering days was teasing a young lass over to a bin of geoducks, those suggestive long-snooted bivalve clams. When she bent over to look in he brought out "Gadzooks," the pet frozen geoduck he kept hidden behind the case, and wiggled it at her. Frozen stiff and hard, his geoduck looked for all the world like a huge male appendage. The lass shrieked and giggled with pleasure and fright as he chased her with it.

The Fishhouse's iced cases were filled with bright tunas and massive, tentacled octopi. I could sense that Deek was feeling a twinge of longing to return to the physical days of slinging thirty-pound fish all day long. I looked down at him and his slowly burgeoning belly, his beard turning white, his stoop. He had a sloppy dignity—powerful, but round.

I took a deep breath and returned to our shared mass of corpuscles. I knew I was still as strong as an ox, even if Deek didn't, but I sensed that I'd better start exercising more.

I felt sort of useless standing there, feeling guilty. An inner voice welled up.

"Focus," it demanded.

I didn't realize that the Deacon in me had vocalized the command, and several people turned and looked at me in surprise. The young monger piped out as he returned his pet geoduck to its lair, "Hey Deek! You okay?"

"It's Deacon," I said unctuously, waving back at him. I turned and moved deeper into the main arcade and didn't look back.

I've never worn a watch, but I could tell the time by seeing that the older, more seasoned shoppers were now doing business at the veggie stalls. It was approaching late afternoon, a time when a lot of vendors lower their prices because their produce is becoming slightly stale; a time when shoppers can haggle.

I watched several of the produce stand vendors breaking down their aisle displays. That's where they display their best stuff, all in precise, intricate patterns. Watching them brought a smile to my heart.

One of the special charms of the Market is watching the ebb and flow of these aisle displays. Stall owners ever so slowly move their displays deeper into the aisle, until management comes by and argues with them to get their displays back behind their lease lines. It's like the tides of the seas—in, out, in, out—revealing the true living, breathing nature of a big-city marketplace. As I walked slowly through this world of crisp commerce, I tried to set in place the elements surrounding Ms. Dahlia.

First the frame. Let's see, I thought, three days ago I save a young lady who was thrown out of a fancy Italian sports car. We fall in love. Her, out of fear, and myself. . . ?

Okay, okay, focus!

She says the guy who threw her out of the car is an East Coast gangster. After three days of bliss, I return to the Market and discover that, indeed, her story has got to be true: the car and the driver check out. He is Ricci Solano, son of a late, so-called mobster who was more of a straight-arrow money manager than a real movie-style gangster. According to the newspapers, son Ricci, however, is a kind of throwback to the mob's Neanderthal days: he beats up his women friends. Next, three jokers enter the deck in the form of three gangster types wearing stingy-brims and their tall leader acts like he's in charge of Ricci as well.

I scratched my head and told myself that those were the givens. My frame.

Now what's the picture? Why does it take such a high powered force to do what they want to do in Seattle? To drive all the way over here from N.Y.C. to find Dahlia?

Cockfights and chicken coops, maybe?

No, no, that's Ricci's thing.

But Seattle is not associated with gangsters. So . . . what, then?

Okay, it's fairly obvious that they are looking for Dahlia as if she holds some sort of secret. But that can't be the main event; that's the negative space on the canvas. Got to be. She's an innocent. Okay, a very street-wise innocent. Nothing she said suggested that she had a hold on Ricci.

A pang of guilt and fear ran through my system and I got the chills. What was it? I racked my brain for an overview. To fill in the blanks.

Was Dahlia a potential embarrassment to the new mob wanting to tone down their act? By the newspaper's accounts, if she were hurt and it became public knowledge, it would be the third strike on Ricci. Bad PR.

Humph: a woman street-waif from the Arctic Circle a threat to one of the most powerful organizations in the country?

Huh? No.

She had conveyed that she had no formal education, but that she learned how to read and write by constantly reading and rereading Nancy Drews. That was one of our bonds; we were both kids at heart.

I smiled inwardly. Dahlia had made very heavy love to me when I showed her my complete mint collection of Hardy Boys mysteries. She had gushed that she wished someone would write a story where Nancy Drew went down on the Hardy Boys. She said it was kind of fitting for today. Boy, was she a Nancy Drew fan!

Oh, oh! One one-thousand, two one-thousand, three one-thousand, four one-thousand . . . five, six, seven, eight, nine, ten . . .

Damn you, Mrs. Alice!

My thoughts were broken by the aroma of fried chicken wafting from the Trump's Chicken Shop across the hall. I lapsed into a trance as my inflamed nostrils led me over to their case of steaming drumsticks.

Just like they did with the girl on the bicycle, Mrs. Alice.

I ordered five from Mr. Kim, the owner. He gripped them one by one with his tongs and put them into a brown paper bag. I quickly paid and immediately pulled out a drum, arched my back, opened my mouth, and lay its crisp, firm body on my tongue. The heat, flavor and texture of its deep-fried crispness made my saliva run. I closed my mouth firmly around the drumstick and greedily pulled the bone out, leaving all the meat and tasty gristle in my mouth. I chewed slowly. My teeth penetrated the skin with a crackle and a hundred thousand tastebuds went to work appeasing the ecstasy and pain of my carbo addiction. Mmm, mmm, mmm . . . I started another drum the same way. Slurp!

By then, several people had stopped and were staring at my quasi-religious rite. What the hey? To a lot of people these days, food's like religion, like sex.

As I chewed, my eye caught the eyes of Pedro, a dump of a streetwise geezer with his starving-dog look. Pedro, a beggar with one leg, never has to utter a word because his look could make a bust of Newt Gingrich spit out a quarter. I handed him the bag of remaining drums and he thanked me by bowing deeply.

The matronly woman who had been staring at me eating came into focus. Perhaps she was recalling some early hard-core experiences. Whatever the reason, as Pedro hopped on she came close and licked her lips.

"Thank you. Thank you for doing that," she said as she melted back into the crowd.

I squared my shoulders as best I could and continued up the main arcade. Through the late afternoon's thinning crowds I saw that Tonk was again setting up for another stint of performing his one-man-band act. His spindly apparatus was almost all set up, and he waved me over. He stood back and looked at it proudly, wanting my reaction.

I looked at it blankly.

"Well?" he asked.

I said it was neat, as always.

Tonk pointed to his new addition, a contrabass harmonica. He had somehow found room for it under the bank of smaller harmonicas. Why hadn't I noticed it at once?

"Fantastic!" I beamed. "Absolutely fantastic!"

He asked if I would watch his masterpiece while he parked his beat-up panel truck.

"Sure," I said. "Do you know a girl named Dahlia?" I added. "She's from the Arctic Circle."

"No," he said, shrugging his shoulders. "What do you mean, from the Arctic Circle?"

I explained that some market musicians had picked her up in Ohio and left her in Montana.

"Maybe she was from Maine," he said helpfully, shrugging his shoulders again. "Or Georgia." He turned to leave.

I began what should have been a five-minute vigil. There was little traffic in the Market. All Tonk had to do was drive the length of Pike Place, turn down Western, enter the Market's parking lot and take the elevator up and back into the main arcade.

On top of his contraption, hanging at odd angles, were two beautiful tail feathers plucked from a scarlet macaw. Tonk had told me earlier that they had been given to him by a member of the Suquamish Tribe above Bainbridge Island. Scarlet macaw feathers were prized, so I kept an eye on them. They looked they had been dipped in blood.

After some time had passed I asked a passerby for the time. She looked at me oddly and pointed up at the huge Market clock. It was 5:30. Tonk had been gone at least fifteen minutes. The crowds were thinning. I began to worry because he had set up for the dinner crowd and they were passing on by. The Market has many top-notch restaurants, so folks with a lot of cash come in. He was missing a prime chance to cadge some bucks.

I pulled out my pipe and unconsciously began the ritual of lighting it. After taking a smoky mouthful of the remains of Ketchikan Pete's stale tobacco, I doubled over, coughing like a fool. I tapped the last of the foul stuff out, looked at the pipe for a long minute, then put it in my mouth unlit. I pulled my cap down tight, jammed my hands deep into my Levi's, and just stared at Tonk's contraption.

As I looked at it, my mind did a weird double-take. I thought I could see Tonk's spirit enter his music machine. It stood there silently as his spirit began to dance. I was frozen in time. I could feel my hair standing on end.

Damn, my sloppy synapses! I tried to pinch myself out of my psychic state, but I couldn't keep from seeing Tonk dancing right smack in front of me.

A young couple walked by with an impish girl of about six in tow. The little girl stopped and looked at the silent machine, then started dancing along with Tonk's spirit. The kid's dad quickly grabbed her and they moved on down toward Le Sojourn. The kid looked back at me.

"Why is that guy so fat, Daddy?" she said. "Daddy, why is that fat man staring at me?

Daddy. . .?"

. . . Actually, I was staring through her, not at her. Through her. Mesmerized by her energy aura—a brilliant white aura.

I blinked and she was gone. But the feeling that Tonk was there persisted. I coughed and shook myself out of my spell.

Focus!

It was getting dark. I was miffed. What was keeping Tonk? Must have been doing some drugs and nodded off a bit, I thought. He was famous for his exotic blends. Tonk was a survivor of the Sixties drug culture. Never got caught, never pushed drugs, but was always experimenting with new concoctions.

I moved out into the street, looked up at the big clock and realized that an hour had gone by. I still clenched my dead pipe in my teeth. A thought surfaced as I wondered if Chief Seattle ever smoked a pipe. My jaw was hurting from clenching the stem. I heard a snap and my tongue felt gravel. I pulled out what remained of the stem, spit out the pieces, and threw the corpse in the gutter.

Damn! I looked back into the market. Most of the day businesses had closed. I put my hands on my hips like MacArthur and gave a great sweeping Look of Eagles down Pike Place.

Wow! Coming up the street were two of the goons. They had a purposeful look about them. I felt naked just standing there. They walked closer.

I felt I had to do something, so I started to play around with Tonk's rig. As I did so, another burst of primal fear showered down my spinal chord. My spinal fluid sizzled. A force was preventing me from touching Tonk's contraption. I was frozen, paralyzed. I had to do something.

I again fell into a trance. I shifted toward Tonk's instruments. A headache began to throb up from the base of my skull. It forced a scrabble word to the surface. I pronounced it out loud.

"Mongolopolase."

The intense headache made me quake with jerky mechanical movements.

I sensed that the two goons had stopped, just inside the shadows of the number one arcade. Just like the next musicians in line do during the day: waiting out of sight until it's their turn to perform. I had to move forward through the wall of mental pain and spiritual trepidation.

Tonk's rig contained several small marachis that he would shake with his head in the rhythms of "Yellow Submarine." I forced myself to try to squeeze his hatband onto my over-large head. When I glanced over my shoulder, sure enough, the goons were eyeing me.

I tried to stuff my oversized gam into the right leg band, which had a cymbal and a series of rubber squeezing horns hanging from it. I jerkingly squeezed a couple of the horns, making like Harpo. I was starting to get nervous; Tonk was very slender and his contraption was far to small for me. A small group of passersby were slowly walking by. One of them yelled out that I must be a drunk.

Voila!

I started acting tipsy. The pain and fear suddenly disappeared. I danced my way out of Tonk's contraption without knocking it over, grabbed the tail feathers, slipped them up my left sleeve, and staggered over to the steps that led into the empty lower levels of the closing Market. I stumbled a bit for good measure.

I hadn't noticed that the goons had anticipated my move to the stairs. In the dusk they came over as if they were old friends.

I did a quick, sweeping turnaround, but not quick enough; one of them turned and lashed out with a cobbler's hammer, grazing my ear. I was lucky; the small tapered hammer could have easily penetrated my temple. No one took any notice of the drama. They just walked on by. Just some buddies trying to help their drunken friend.

I recoiled and flashed back on an old pulp detective novel I'd read at fifteen. The hammer, as a weapon, causes the victim to appear drunk, with very little bloody damage. The attackers can lead away their "buddy," who has "drunk too much," while the victim is slowly dying. It gives goons time to ask questions before their victim dies.

The other goon had hold of my sweatshirt, but the momentum of my weight pulled me away from him. I staggered into the street, making a Camaro cowboy with his Ms. Peroxide slam on the brakes and horn. The mudflap's hooter didn't realize that his Camaro separated me from the goons and saved my life. The close call slammed all my synapses to attention.

Total focus!

I stumbled across the street on all fours and crabwalked into the entrance of the Corner Market Building. Early evening sports pointed and laughed at me, the drunk. Ha, ha, ha! I righted myself in the foyer and looked down the dark steps on my right that led to Jazzim's, featuring Big Shirley.

"Saint Louie woman. . . ." wailed Shirley's full, rich voice.

". . . with all her diamond rings," I hummed as I went by Geni's Meats. I flashed on the past. This was the site of the old horse-meat butcher . . .

I need a horse, I thought. Horse meat?

Shirley sang on: "She leads her man around, by her apron strings. . . ."

I was in the shadows of the Corner Market between the meat place and the Chinese basket shop.

In the distance Shirley lamented, "If it wasn't for powder . . ."

I looked back and saw the silhouettes of the goons. They were looking at the three ways they could go: up, down or straight ahead toward me. I felt a dribble of ooze running down the left side of my neck. I brushed at it and tasted the wetness on my fingers. It was blood from the attack with the hammer. It made my legs rubbery and I swayed as Shirley wailed.

"That gadabout, wouldn't've got no place . . ."

Barber college . . . This had been a barber college at one time.

". . . no place, no place . . ."

A riff of a bass guitar twang reverberated from above.

"Little Bill and The Blue Notes," I thought. "They were Diane Schuur's band when she first sang upstairs in the Bar and Grill."

In my partial shock, I was going over the spiel I use when I take someone for a tour of the Market. Fortunately, the spell was broken when I slipped on a greasy newspaper and banged into a display case. The noise alerted the goons and they came running. I cursed The Crab House as I stumbled. I smelled fish in the darkness.

Fish and chips in newspapers, my ass.

As I kicked the paper away from my foot I heard the welcome sound of a rhythmic clatter. I ran toward it. It was the sound of metal shopfront shutters being rolled down for the night. Julio was just pulling on the last one in a series of five that ran along the length of the building.

I slid onto my back and squiggled out of the darkness and under the shutters. Julio jumped back, swearing in his native Tagalog. My belly stopped the shutter's descent as I slithered under.

The security sergeant, who'd seen everything that could possibly happen in a big city, quickly regained his composure. It wasn't unusual for him to find people locked into the Market for the night.

Julio laughed. "Deacon, what are you doing in there?"

I was about to tell them about the goons but checked myself. Instead I lied.

"I fell asleep at the Malaysian Cafe. Julio, are the other shutters being shut down? The one at the front of the building?" I pointed back through where I'd entered.

"Jane's doing them right now. Deacon, you got to stop eating so much. Your belly almost broke that shutter. And it looks like you scratched your ear on it. Want a bandaid?"

"No, it's nothing."

"It's your ear," Julio said, snapping the padlock in place. He moved on up Pike Place.

"Grassy-ass Julio," I yelled out to him. "Thanks ever so much."

"That's 'gracias,' Deacon," Julio replied in a flawless Oxford accent. He grinned.

I removed Tonk's feathers from my sleeve and checked them. They were undamaged from all my activity. I looked into the gloom behind the shutters and quickly moved up Post Alley in the opposite direction from Julio. I turned right at the next street and made my way up to First Avenue. There, I made another right and returned to Pike. I crossed the street and carefully looked over at the shutter just inside the foyer of the Corner Market Building.

Sure as rain, the two goons were trapped inside.

I passed the phone booth just down from Pike and stopped. No, I wasn't looking for the spot where Woody Guthrie was arrested for busking in the forties.

Focus!

I went back to the phone booth and called Market Security. Jane answered on her portable, so I disguised my voice and told her there were a couple of suspicious characters locked in the Corner Market Building. Jane was a to-the-letter type, and if it was up to her these two would be charged with trespassing. Then I realized that Julio was more worldly, and he was in charge. Well, it was a fifty-fifty chance that they would go to jail.

I continued down First, made a right at Dope Dealin' Alley, then continued up lower Post Alley. If it was past ten it would be dangerous for me to be in this location because I hate dope dealers and they know it. Their brand of evil action doesn't start till later in the night.

I huffed and puffed back up to Bugsy's. Stopped. After I gained my breath I decided to climb the little stairs to the main arcade and see what the result of my phone call had been.

I crept up the steps; at eye level I stopped and peered up to the main arcade. I could see Jane and Julio questioning the two goons.

I looked over Tonk's contraption; nothing had changed. It was still in its place waiting for Tonk to return. I froze when I heard somebody huffing and puffing behind me. As the sounds got louder, I turned around and looked back down Post Alley.

Rounding the corner, out of breath, came Jeanie, a craftsperson I had known for some time. She didn't see me. She frantically looked behind her, then broke into a run up First Avenue.

I watched her disappear across the street. She was crossing against the light, and several cars honked their horns. Seeing Jeanie at this hour disturbed me, so I thought I had better get down to Bugsy's, pronto. Bad moon rising and all that.

Jeanie is as straight as folks come these days. I met her several years ago and we went out a few times. Through the years we drifted apart, but we're still friends. She has a going business on the craft line selling brooms she makes by hand. Brouha's Brooms. That's her company's name. Means the witch's broom. She's easy going, with a great sense of humor, so seeing her down there in such a state had me really worried. It was completely out of character.

She had gotten married a few years back and had a couple of very young kids who needed her constant attention 'cause she lives on a houseboat across town.

Hmmm. I remembered that she had a taste for the booze, but never dope. So why the hell should she be running from Dope Dealin' Alley at eleven at night? I scratched my head on that one. Damn, everything seemed out of kilter.

I looked back at Julio. Jane had become animated, and she looked like she wanted to run them in. Go Jane! But Julio was in charge, and I knew he would let them go after a complete report was made.

I turned, slipped back down the narrow steps, and moved through the tunnel toward the alcove where Bugsy's main entrance is. As I was about to enter, a hoarse, authoritative voice told me to freeze. I froze.

From out of the shadows emerged Jesse Hallsey, a semi-retired plainclothes cop working the narcotics beat. We knew each other well.

Jesse is a very big man. He was also wearing three-inch-heel cowboy boots and a huge Russian fur cap. The ensemble took his height to well over seven feet. He was ex-NFL. Used to play on the line of the Dallas Cowboys. He was also wearing his signature trenchcoat, which made him look like he was straight out of the movies. Pity the petty hood who crossed him.

I'd had my share of his bad humor through the years. He was a drinker, and when he stopped you for something he tried everything possible to bait you so he could run you in.

But there was an upside with this downside. Jesse was fair, and the mere fact of his presence at the Market kept the place free of the hoods which have infested other parts of downtown. My run-ins with him had been many, usually because I had been drinking too much myself. He had once tried to backhand me in his office, but I ducked, and he slammed his hand into a hard frame that held his graduation papers from the L.A. Police Academy. I ran on out of there. The next day, he had his arm in a cast.

That had happened five years ago, but he hadn't forgotten it. Later, he had tried to arrest me for fighting when I broke up an argument between two thugs who were throwing punches over who owned a can of mackerel they had shoplifted from Tanvy's Grocery. Actually, we ended up on the same side in that tense situation, and he must have found some grudging respect for me 'cause he has laid off my case since then.

Jess had one hell of a difficult job keeping the peace on the streets. That made him constantly on edge. I respected him, because, like me, he had an overview.

The one thing I had learned through the years was to not be intimidated by him. I was bone weary and getting pissed off. I wanted sleep. His long arm was raised, and he held his hand wide open for emphasis.

"Deek, did you just come up the alley?"

"No, I was just coming down those steps," I answered, pointing back at the stairway.

Jess looked over my shoulder at the steps. "I just saw you walk down the dealin' alley and up Post!" he said authoritatively.

I was tired and not about to argue. "Okay, technically you're right. That's the way I came up a few minutes ago. Then I had second thoughts and came back down here, and then you stopped me."

"Why?" he said accusingly.

Well, he had me there. I had to think up an answer real quick.

"Why did you stop me?" I ad-libbed.

He looked at me as if to say: Try again.

"I was going to have another drink before I went home," I continued, "so I first looked up to see if the Pike Bar was open. Then I was going to see if Bugsy's was open.

"Look, my scoot is just around the corner; it's cold; I need to warm up before I ride to the ferry."

Jess leaned deep down and smelled my breath. "You ain't been drinking," he said. His eyes were staring deep into me, just baiting me to show some guilt. I didn't bite.

Was I innocent? Guilty? What was the use; I was both.

"Okay, Jess," I said, "you've got me dead to rights. Take me in. I've had a rough day. I'm tired. I need some sleep."

He just stared at me. "You're guilty," he said.

"No I'm not," I answered in a tiny little guilt-ridden voice.

"Come with me," he said, taking my arm.

Man, I was getting pissed. Now I had talked myself into getting arrested. But instead of walking me up to his office, we walked back down Post Alley. At Dope Dealin' Alley he grabbed my arm and escorted me up the steps. He was taking me back the way I had come. I hoped he wasn't going to take me up on First, thinking that the goons would spot me. We stopped at the first landing. It served as an entryway to an architect's studio.

"I was standing in there when you walked by," he said, flicking on his flashlight.

The first thing I saw was a bright yellow strip of policeman's tape that's used to rope off the crime scene. He lowered his flash and aimed it on a pool of thick blood.

I gagged.

Jess was matter-of-fact as he moved the beam of light around the pool of blood.

"Would you look at that. . . . Absolutely no smear or droplets other than this one, an almost perfectly round pool. It's as if the body was held in a body bag and drained. Like completely drained. Like maybe what was left just floated away. What do you think happened?"

"Me? Why do you ask me?"

"Well, it certainly is a coincidence, seeing you walk by, the way you hate pushers. It makes you kind of a suspect, Deek, old boy."

Boy, Jess loved to exaggerate.

"I ain't about to kill someone," I told him coolly. "When did you ever see me fighting?"

He laughed. "When you whipped those two shoplifters with that octopus."

"Okay, Jess, that was a long time ago. I had to do that; you know it. I had to stop them quick 'cause they were knocking down our crab displays. Look, what's so unusual about seeing blood in this place?" I sagged. "I'm so tired, Jess. Tomorrow I'll put my ear to the streets. Maybe something will turn up."

He looked at me with his menacing eyes. "Who ran up the alley? They must have passed you."

"Didn't see anybody," I lied.

"The person came out of the shadows down below and shined a light up here. It must have shown who I was, and the person took off." I said nothing.

He shined his flash straight into my eyes. "After all these years, you still wear your guilt on your sleeve. You're an idiot. Get out of here."

I rapidly walked back up Post Alley, wondering why I didn't tell him Jeanie's name. Maybe it wasn't her. Maybe, maybe . . . I looked back over my shoulder before I turned into Bugsy's foyer.

"It's a free country," I mumbled loudly, to no one. "Dammit, Jess, I've got my rights. I can feel guilty if I want, dammit. Besides, in America if someone wants to kill someone it's all right as long as they're willing to pay the price."

I guiltily looked over my shoulder again and dashed into the foyer. The last thing I wanted Jess to know was that I slept there on occasion.

Lea and Antonio had left without leaving the outside light on, so I had to feel through my keys until I found the one for Bugsy's. It seemed like a long time until I found the right key.

Chapter 10

Focus

"Dum, dum . . . speak softly, Baby, dadada, da, be doo doo . . ."

I UNLOCKED THE DOOR and entered Bugsy's. With a deep breath, I gathered my thoughts and made my way in the darkness over to the corner where my "office" was located. I forced my mind to regroup. Dammit! My escape from the two thugs had been lucky. But why were they after me in the first place? I felt useless as a vacuum tube.

My only direct link to them had been earlier in the afternoon when I peeked into their Aerostar. Yet that didn't figure; it was their leader who had confronted me.

I decided to keep the lights off, so I had to maneuver in the semi-darkness and stubbed my toe on a chair. At the salad bar, where my sea chest was stored, I bent down slowly, feeling a slight twinge of pain from my crusty verts—*vertebrae, dammit!* I opened the cabinet below and took out my sleeping bag and limp air mattress.

I flopped the dead mattress down, located the air valve by touch, and began inflating it by mouth. After twenty minutes of huffing and puffing, I managed to get it partially filled. I placed it between the tables, unrolled the sleeping bag, and laid it over the mattress. Wearily, I undressed and carefully arranged my clothes on the backs of a couple of the chairs. I kept my briefs on.

I plunked Tonk's feathers in a vase of dried flowers. I had gained some energy and I started prancing. Ever since I was a little kid, something has come over me whenever I take my clothes off: I want to dance striptease-like. Never saw a show till I was a teenager, so it must be a natural urge.

I did a raunchy go-go dance over to the bar, humming "tutti frutti," while my belly jiggled to the rhythms I created. A hundred pounds or so ago, I had been a snappy dancer. Since I couldn't sing loud because that might attract Jess, I hummed under my breath.

I bumped and ground over to the fridge and pulled out the fixings for a Dagwood sandwich, then went to the counter and found two stale rolls. The grill was still warm, so I turned it back on and put the buns on to soften them.

I backed up to the mirror in front of the bar and flexed my arm muscles. I muttered, "Grrrr!" After admiring my pecs a while, I turned, opened the fridge, looked for a Kemper, but settled on a bottle of Ballard Bitter.

"Buns, buns, bee he done, de doo doo," I hummed.

I strutted back to the grill to check on the toasting rolls. They were still on the tough side so I removed them, doused them with beer and put them back on, mashing them a bit with my palms. The grill's heat caused them to spit and sputter, but in less than 10 seconds, the fragrant steam did its job and the buns were as soft as Dahlia's. I took them off and smeared some mayonnaise and mustard on them—like I would Dahlia's—but that's where the two sets of delightful buns separated.

Yuk, yuk! Oh the puns de doo doo . . .

I grabbed four different types of cold cuts, scrunched them up, slapped them on and held them in place with slabs of three different types of sliced cheese. I'd learned to scrunch up cold cuts rather than just lay them flat in the deli in West Hollywood where Melrose Place branches off Melrose. Scrunching them allows their flavors to breathe.

I added a mound of finely chopped olives, some capers, onions, two anchovies. As I poured on Bugsy's secret hot green olive sauce, I realized I was making myself a pizza on a roll—a rock and roll . . . I took a deep swig of the Bitter, then put my concoction on a plate and ambled over to the window, where I eased into a well-used Windsor bowback. From my seat I could see out over moonlit Elliott Bay. The harbor was still except for a huge freighter gliding silently to the APL berths just south of the Kingdome. Damn boat seemed to be two thousand feet long.

I had to concentrate on the sandwich because I'd made it so big. It took some doing, but I finally got one edge of it between my teeth and bit down into pure heaven.

Unfortunately, while I chewed, my eyes wandered down six stories to Waterway Avenue and hell: my canyon of dark brick walls, forbidding in the night. Far below, I could faintly see the outline of the dead seagull. A hooded shopping-cart streetperson, dressed in rags, slowly plodded over it. His cart was empty, but I knew that it would be full by daybreak. Chills went up my spine.

After two bites I lost my appetite. I opened the window a few inches. The cold sea breeze rushed in, reviving my spirits a bit. The air was brisk.

I was angry. Why did Waterway Avenue have that effect on me? By day it's okay? But at night?

My mind free-associated and looped back to Dahlia. It was weird: ever since she had entered my life everything seemed painfully clear, maybe even directed in some way. This thought was disturbing, and the cold breeze made me shiver.

I placed the remains of my sandwich on the sill and closed the window, a little too hard. I drained the glass, got up, walked over to the sink and washed my plate. I turned off the grill, hovering there a bit to warm up. Then I went to the main counter, took the portable phone off its holder, turned if off, and brought it over to my makeshift bed and crawled in.

The sleeping bag was made of goose down and was as comfy as they come. It was one of the most expensive models on the market. First Avenue, just south of the Market, was an Alaska outfitting paradise. Everything for the outdoorsman: rubber rafts, shovels. Yessiree!

I heard a swooping sound, then some heavy shuffling and scraping. My instincts forced me to look over to the front door. I peered through the glass, trying to see through the gloom. Then I realized what it was and turned back to the window.

Outside, Georgette was wrestling with the hefty leftovers I'd left on the sill, doing battle with two other gulls that had arrived. I laughed when the three of them managed to shove the mighty morsel over the side and the trio took off after their treasure. As hungry as they were, I knew the sandwich would never make it to the ground.

I snuggled deep into the sleeping bag. Once I was settled in I turned on the phone and punched in the *Exacto's* number in the hope that Dahlia had returned. As the phone rang I started to think of sweet baby Dahlia and Paul began to swell. I grabbed old Paul with my left hand as I held the phone with my right, in anticipation.

"Focus," I uttered out loud.

It seemed my hands were full for the longest time, but then my answering machine kicked in. After the beep, I held the phone disappointedly while old Paul wilted like an over-warm candle. Damn, just when I could go for some uninterrupted stroking, the beast within me fails.

Damn you, Mrs. Alice!

A muffled voice repeated, "If you want to make a call. . . ." I pulled the phone out from under the sleeping bag and turned it off.

Focus!

My thoughts floated around a bit, then focused on Tonk. How could he leave his prize creation and disappear?

It was just like a hundred times before, I thought; the same routine: I stop and help him set up his one-man-band, then I watch it while he parks his van in the garage. This time I ask if he knows a girl named Dahlia. He says he doesn't. When I mention that she told me she had been picked up in Ohio he acts as if it happens all the time. That means it could have happened.

Was another piece of the puzzle falling into place? Dahlia said she'd been stranded in Montana. That, and the maps in Ricci's car. But Tonk wasn't involved. So?

Thinking back, I realized the hoods didn't know that. All Ricci knew was that Dahlia knew some Market street musicians. Tonk was by far the most known musician on Pike Place, so they would naturally focus on him. A light went on just behind the ear that had been grazed by the cobbler's hammer. They would want to question him.

Damn! Ouch!

I cupped my ear in frustration. It hurt, but I kept my focus.

Boy, was I dull-witted. Why didn't I think about that last evening? The reason why Tonk never made it back was because he had been questioned by the goons with their wicked hammer.

Damn, damn, damn!

And Tonk maybe told them that I was asking the same questions. Me, the guy who was watching his music machine. No wonder they knew who I was. They came back, saw me, attacked me; I escaped; they came after me.

It made perfect sense. Except what happened to Tonk.

Tonk's a survivor, I rationalized.

I found the phone and dialed Market Security. Julio was still on duty. I told him that Tonk had left for the night.

"Julio," I asked, "could you keep Tonk's rig in your office for the night?"

"Sure, Deacon" he said. "By the way, did you know that there were two other gentlemen locked into the Corner Market Building tonight?"

"No," I replied, playing dumb.

"Yeah, they said they were trying to find Jazzim's, walked right by it, and ended up in the Corner Market."

"Some people!" I said. I nervously laughed and hung up. I tried to reach the *Exacto* again. No answer. I sighed.

I tried to sleep, but my mind was traveling a mile a minute. Something was burning just on the edge of my awareness.

Was I exaggerating everything? Were mobsters from the East Coast actually out to kill people? What in the world would attract the mob to the Pike Place Market? This was a community of artists, small business owners, farmers. Ricci searching for his ladyfriend made some sense, but what did the three stingy-brims want? It just didn't figure. As I strained for solutions, my overloaded synapses gave out on me and I lapsed into a loose-jointed dream.

I was in bed and had to burp badly, but I was hung up. I tried and tried, and then the burp arrived with a vengeance. It was a huge blast that rattled the ceiling of my dream. In the dream, I woke to see the goons swimming after Dahlia, who was in a shopping cart, being pulled by a flock of fighting cocks chasing my old dog, Mushroom, down the Pacific Coast Highway . . .

Dahlia is nude and flaunting her sexuality, laughing hysterically. The goons turn into skaters in green uniforms who glide down Pike Place, showering the street with parking tickets, causing all the cars along the street to disappear. Behind them rolls the huge green Lamborghini. The car fills up the whole street.

The door opens and Ricci rises out of it, at least fifty feet into the air. He reaches over the three mobsters, plucks tiny Dahlia from the grocery cart, and throws her into the Lamborghini's seat. The giant Ricci slides back into his car, settles in beside Dahlia, and shuts the door.

The dream takes me through the car's windshield of dark, Hollywood glass. Ricci has shrunk to normal size and Dahlia, beside him, is aggressively tearing off his pants and pulling out his rigid cock. She then works a diamond-studded cock ring off of it. She kisses the ring, then puts it on her wrist.

Ricci places a matching necklace over Dahlia's head, and then she goes down on him. Ricci jams her head down hard on his cock. It gets larger and larger until it chokes her. She begins to gag and struggle. He holds her down and grabs the necklace like she is a bucking bronco.

"Get it on, girlie, giddyup!" he yells, pulling on the necklace.

The green car becomes a green field and Ricci is wearing a cowboy hat. He grips Dahlia's hair and necklace. She writhes in a stooped-over death dance. He climaxes, breaking her neck, and she dies instantly. His sweaty face leers at me.

"Man, dis is better 'n fuckin' dem Montana chickens in the ass!" he yells. Then he spots me looking in and lashes out with a cobbler's hammer . . .

I woke up and sat bolt upright, covered in sweat. My hands were clenched so hard I had lost all feeling in them. I was gulping. I staggered up and stumbled over to the counter and poured myself a glass of water. My stomach ached and was cramping. I poured myself another glass, then went down to the bathroom and vomited.

Afterward, I sat on the toilet for what must have been an hour. Then, in a trance, I edged up the steps and slumped in the Windsor, staring out at the bay.

The hot sauce, I thought, too much hot sauce.

Eventually, I fell asleep.

My eyes were closed, but I sensed the morning light coming in through my eyelids. I heard a soft tapping in front of me and slowly opened my eyes. Georgette was outside the window waiting for a handout.

I'd not moved during the night, so when I tried to get up I felt as rigid as a piece of well-seasoned wood. Georgette stood there staring at me like I was her servant. I stupidly stared back, but she stared me down. She was one demanding bitch.

I stiffly got up and stretched. I walked to the counter and located some more stale buns, took one back, opened the window and gave it to the gull. The open window allowed in the morning's fresh salt air, and I inhaled deeply.

Georgette flapped off with the bun. Her powerful wings propelled her gracefully up to her nest on the roof, six stories higher. The sun glinted on her feathers and carried my eyes back out into the bay where the morning ferry from the island was crossing to the city. I glanced over at the wall clock and saw that it was the 7:10 boat.

I reached down, grabbed the phone and tried to dial. Dead. I had turned it on in my tossing and turning, draining the battery. I shook my head in annoyance and looked around. The previous evening's events came back to me.

I went to the desk and replaced the phone on its cradle charger, then returned to the Windsor. I sat down and pondered on my life-long cycle of goofy by day, nightmares by night. A circus clown could identify with that. A clown that blew up ballons into funny, loved creatures. Bloated, filled-with-air creatures that could instantly pop and disappear. Spent latex. Useless and ugly as a used condom.

I turned back to the phone. I hoped it would be ready when Lia came in at ten. I got up and went to the bathroom and took a long pee, then went over to the sink, splashed water over my face and looked in the mirror.

The lines around the eyes were deeper. The hair was scrabbly and shooting out in different directions. The eyes were still mine, but vacant and tired. I filled a towel with water and wrapped my head in it.

Ahhhhhh . . .

Some pink returned to my skin, but my eyes were trying to tell me of a loss. I dried myself, patted my hair, and went back upstairs, resolved to keep a focus. I couldn't phone home until I got dressed and went outside.

I rolled up the sleeping gear, stuffed it back in the chest of drawers and slowly dressed. I looked around and cleaned up, putting things back in place. I took Tonk's feathers and placed them neatly in my sea chest.

By chance, I looked out the window where I'd tossed the sandwich to Georgette the previous night. The window sill was greasy, so I walked over to the counter, grabbed a wet rag, reopened the window and mopped it off.

The sea breeze and the warm rays of the sun helped revitalize me. I took several deep breaths and began to feel better. After a final look around I pulled out my wallet, grabbed a twenty, opened the fridge and placed it on the rack that held the remaining cold cuts.

Antonio would know it was from me, and everything would be explained. They knew that, from time to time, I got drunk—I mean slightly askew. Okay, from time to time I got tipsy at the La Gala next door and slept over at Bugsy's. No big deal—as long as I cleaned up.

I left and climbed the severe steps back up to the main arcade. Tonk's rig was gone, but I was still nervous from the night before.

I made for the phone in a little-known section of the Market known as the atrium. If Ricci's goons were up and about, combing the market, that would be the last place they'd look.

I turned left and slunk down to the Indian antique store, called The Thunderbird, then across the Bridge of Cries over Post Alley. On my right, Tillie was getting ready to open her cafe. The smell of fresh-brewed coffee wafted out of her establishment.

I made it to the bank of phones across from Watercolors Fresh Daily's stand, stuffed a quarter in the slot, and dialed the *Exacto*.

No answer. The answering machine came on: "I'm a Yankee Doodle Dandy . . ."

This time I left a message: "It's me again. Just hold tight."

I held the phone for a whole minute, then hung up. I felt defeated. I knew she wasn't there, I just knew it. She was with the cruelest type of criminal on earth. A person who took love and gave pain in return. If the newspapers were true, a sadist. Worse, a spoiled rich-kid sadist.

I opened the phone book and located the number of The Grand Hotel. I stuffed in another quarter and dialed. I got a connection and asked for Mr. Solano's room. The clerk replied crisply that Mr. Solano had left instructions not to be disturbed. Using an overbearing tone, I asked if he had requested a wake-up call.

"No," she replied, just as crisply.

"It's very important," I told her.

"If it's that important, then I'm sure Mr. Solano will contact you when he wakes up. Goodbye."

I stood there in frustration. I replaced the receiver and slouched out to the main arcade, then back to Tillie's.

Her place looked inviting, as always. I hesitated a moment, then decided to move on. I wondered if I should just forget the whole thing. They were back together and it was simply all over. I reasoned that the goons had been brought in to find her for Ricci.

They found her and it's over, I thought. I shrugged my shoulders, lost my fear, and walked down toward Dunhill's. I figured that, since it was all over, I'd never see Ricci and the goons again.

They're on their way back to New York, I thought. Probably in Spokane right now. I felt a huge emptiness in my stomach as I sorted out the ramifications. He has her, I thought, but will he take care of her? No, he'll beat on her.

I tried to recall the details of what the newspaper articles had reported about his past relationships. It was a blur.

I thought of my cat, Tart. How long did it take her to toy with a mouse before she killed it? Two, three hours?

Let's see, a cat . . .

Shit!

It was so unfathomable because . . . because she came from nowhere. No one knew her. Where was Tonk; where had they both gone?

I walked back to the arcade, nodding to just about everyone I passed. I moved by some craft people setting up and wedged through a flock of early morning tourists taking pictures of the farmers. Some of them wore tags stuck to their coats that said they were from Des Moines, Iowa. They were stout and full of corn-fed vitality. I instantly liked them.

I moved on over the skybridge and took the elevator down to the parking lot on the other side of Waterway Avenue.

I was wary. I got off on the top floor and worked myself down five flights of parking stalls, looking for Tonk's van. I found what I wanted on the second floor. It was unlocked.

I opened the door and noticed that the key was still in the van. I stepped up inside to see if Tonk was in there asleep. There was no evidence that anyone had spent the night. I looked around to see if anything had been stolen; everything was in place. I knew where Tonk held his stash of his famous blends; it was behind the dashboard on the passenger side.

I reached up behind the glove box and pulled down a well-used cigar box that was sitting on its specially made shelf. I opened it and surveyed the paraphernalia.

There was a bag of classic dry sinsemilla, which I understood was the base for most of his blends. There was a small bag of white powder I assumed to be cocaine. Also, there was a pack of Pall Malls.

I looked closely at the tips of the cigarettes and knew that these were the legendary Hits he was famous for. Hits were normal cigarettes dipped into liquefied marijuana, popular in the Sixties. Tonk called them Hits because it takes only one inhaling to blast a doper to the upper reaches of a high. The scuttlebutt was that he took out a copyright on the name.

I decided to take the box of dope so that if the cops were to search his van they wouldn't find anything. I removed the keys from the ignition and placed them on the floorboards, then got out, closed the door and made my way back up to the Market.

Tonk must have been loaded and got lost. Easy to do in the Market; it's like a maze. Get a little drunk or high and you could get lost forever.

He's probably sleeping it off somewhere, I told myself. Maybe the goons questioned him and beat him up, so he's sleeping it off.

I remembered the cobbler's hammer and shuddered.

I passed behind the bank of dumpsters that the garbage attendants were rolling along to the first floor and the waiting garbage truck. They were painted the same sickly green shade as the Lamborghini, the same shade the garbage guys wore.

The elevator door opened and I entered. I got off at Waterway Avenue, avoiding the sky bridge seven floors above just in case I was being followed. I was overly jumpy.

Why? The goons were gone; Tonk would show up. Okay, maybe I wouldn't see Dahlia again. Still, I figured it was best to play it safe.

I jaywalked across Waterway Avenue and headed to another elevator that I knew would take me up behind the Trump's Chicken Shop. That would give me time to see who was on the main floor before I entered. I passed Bradley, who was on his way to open his reptile shop just down the avenue.

A perfect business for Waterway Avenue, I thought. Reptiles.

The elevator took forever to arrive. I should have expected it, for the baker often used it to bring baked goods from his fourth floor bakery up to Fat Baker's this time of day. The smell of his fresh bread was making me salivate. It was another five minutes before it arrived.

I rode up alone. I tensed up when the light came on denoting that someone wanted the elevator on the third lower level, Herc's level. It wasn't a rational reaction, but that's how edgy I'd become. *Focus!*

I forced myself to accept that danger had passed. I fantasized that the handsome young New Yorker got his lady, and he and his buddies had ridden off into the sunset—sunrise, rather—to his Isle of Manhattan. I was the dirty garage attendant who had fixed the flat tire on his fancy car so they could move on. Later, I would be stiffed by his bum check for my efforts.

The elevator door opened and two teenage boys got on. Their faces were dotted with pimples and their eyes were vacant from watching too much MTV.

I got out and went to the head of the stairs in the center of the third level and peered over at Hercules' fortune-telling studio. I had a wild thought that he could help me again. I could say I was his agent, and the pair of us could go over to The Grand and beat the shit out of Ricci before he left town. Hercules was a gentle as a lamb unless . . .

"Go get Ken," I'd say.

I shrugged. They wouldn't let Herc get within a block of the hotel.

I got another idea. I decided that I'd go to The Grand myself and talk to Ricci if he was still there. I'd take the newspaper article and tell him to lay off Dahlia.

As I climbed the next set of stairs to the lower level's mezzanine, I steeled myself for the task; I was growing bolder. At the same time I realized I was also hungry as hell, so when I reached the main arcade I went into Dunhill's for breakfast. I went upstairs to the cozy, second-floor bar, as I usually do in the morning.

Bea, the bartender, smiled and waved. She is one of the main reasons I go there. She always has a smile on her face. My favorite

perch is the nook area behind the bar where you can look down along
the main arcade.

I eased into the first booth and opened the sliding window as
far as it would go, so I could lean out. Market customers below were
beginning to filter in for the day's shopping. The morning is the best
time to shop, before the hordes of visitors arrive and fill the place to
a point where no one can move—at least not comfortably.

Bea walked over to take my order.

"Hot coffee," I said, "corned beef hash, two sunnysides, straight
up on top and staring at me like those Marilyn Monroe titties on that
calendar of hers."

She laughed. She'd heard this line many times before.

As Bea returned to the bar, I remembered the first time I saw
the calendar. It was on the wall of a winery I had snuck into on a
weekend when I was a little kid. The sun was glaring through the
little windows high up above the huge vats of wine. It had been a
hot day. The winery was on a hill above Montecito. The view of the
ocean stretched for miles.

I had wandered through the cool, concrete building following
pipes and climbing stairways. I came to a cramped office high up
above the main floor. The little window was filled with sunlight, and
a beam directed my eye to the calendar. Rays of sunlight shone
through the dirty window, illuminating the picture like some old re-
ligious painting.

Marilyn was a beauty. Her eyes were so open . . . her body so
voluptuous . . . Everything about her was so feminine. She was so
fresh and vital. Not like . . .

Mrs. Alice, eat your heart out.

My recollection was broken by Bea's arrival with my full plate
of hash and eggs. Bea smiled, for she knew my thought patterns. She
placed the plate in front of me and handed me the morning paper.

I stared down at the jiggling, giggling yokes flopped teasingly on top of the steaming hash. I swear those eggs were alive and taunting me to gobble them up. I held the trusty morning newspaper—the P.I.—as though it were a utensil, then froze and looked up into Bea's laughing eyes. I opened my mouth to call her a wise guy, but it was too filled with saliva, so I sort of sputtered as I asked her what was so funny. She doubled over and laughed. She collected herself and came up behind me, and gave both my shoulders a deep pinch.

"Nothing's the matter," she said. "Everything's as it should be."

I grunted and she left.

I placed the newspaper on the table, scanning the front page for pics and headlines. The P.I. was famous for putting weird headlines close to public figures, like "Drag queens busted in Queen Anne Park" close to a picture of Hillary and Janet Reno smiling for the adoring masses.

I carefully unfolded the napkin, tucking an edge under the collar of my sweatshirt. The napkin formed a huge white diamond. I looked down at my girth and wondered why my belly seemed so much larger. I shrugged my shoulders and thought that it was a combination of the white of the napkin, and that it was puffing up, preparing itself for the tasty, steaming hash.

Well, I dug in, straight through the yokes, with a knife in my right hand and a fork in my left, slicing and hauling out a heaping portion just dripping with yoke juice. It entered my mouth like a dream come true, and I chewed slowly. I looked down at the plate and the mound remaining, yoke drooling down its sides. It looked like magma on an active Hawaiian volcano. I looked over at the edge of the bar's mirror and saw my reflection. There was a gleam in my eyes. I swallowed and gave a fine Look of Eagles.

I saluted myself, then turned back and dove in with relish.

Part II

Deacon Takes Over

Chapter 11

Corned Beef & Aerostars

". . . down at the house . . . the house of blue lights . . ."

ABOUT TWENTY MINUTES LATER, after my last bite, I leaned back, satiated. I missed my old pipe, and absently waved my hand, puffing-like, as though in a dream. Bea came over, handed me a Marlboro, and brought out a lighter. I lit up and took a puff. I don't inhale, but I like the effect of smoking: the movements, the style, the smoke curling up as I melt down.

I glanced at the sports section. There was really nothing there that interested me. I'm a football fan and was out of season. I looked down at the crowds of shoppers swirling around the veggie stalls. The scene reminded me of a Mark Tobey painting, the ones splashed with color and movement. They were amazing paintings, but nothing beats the real thing. The scene made me realize why I decided on my vocation.

The Market was so rich in life and the intensity of living it. Market folks needed people around with a sense of overview, however skewed. I mean, I didn't really know if my overview was any better than anyone else's. That wasn't the point. The point was to have an overview and stick by it.

I was justifying so much that I almost missed seeing the distinctive side panel of the dusty Aerostar visible through one of the back stall windows that a farmer had opened. As it cruised slowly by I glimpsed a piece of the New York State license plate and tensed up, like a beginning dart player throwing for the first time. "Now what the hell?" I almost shouted. I nervously stubbed out the cigarette, grabbed the bill and went to pay.

Bea took my money but looked as though she wondered what was wrong. I flashed her a cockeyed smile and mumbled something about a meeting. She looked concerned and said that Alex from the fried chicken shop had asked her to remind me to come to the Design and Review Committee meeting today.

"He said it was important," she said.

I nodded and told her that I'd talk to him. She admonished me sweetly and told me that she had witnessed my promise that I would attend.

As I left, I tried to recall the moment. It came back to me in segments. We had been drinking pretty heavily several nights ago, and he had cried about unfair competition. I remembered that, indeed, I had promised him that I would attend, but would judge the situation for myself. I had hinted that the Market had millions of visitors a year and that, just maybe, there was room for another chicken shop. He didn't like what I said, but we parted on good terms.

As I walked down to the main arcade I had another idea. I snapped my fingers as I backtracked up to Dunhill's third level.

Beth was at the bar, serving another customer. Everyone else was either reading newspapers or watching the TV sitting high up in a far corner. I didn't know what my plan of action would be, but I reassured myself with a "so far, so good" attitude.

I detoured to the men's room and used the toilet for a long time. Bugsy's hot sauce from the previous night still burned my insides, but, all in all, it was a good crap. I washed my hands slowly and thoroughly, like a surgeon getting ready for action.

I left the bathroom and went across the room to see if the little-known stairwell that led straight down to the arcade was open. It was.

I closed the door and scanned the long dining room that overlooked the bay. There was just one couple at the other end, but they were deeply involved in conversation. I followed the wall to another door that led to the roof.

I was still carrying Tonk's cigar box, so I removed the dope, tore up the box and stuffed the pieces into the waste can next to the door. I tested the door to make sure it opened from the outside. It did. To be sure it stayed open, I wedged a flattened 7-Up can between it and the doorwell.

I went outside on to the roof and moved down the narrow walkway that was lined by huge flower pots filled with big, squat, red geraniums. The pots were enormous and looked hard to move. Barry, the Market's head custodian, loved flowers, so the place was filled with them. I carefully made my way along the pathway, looking between the flowers down at the parked cars. I spotted the Aerostar just ahead and moved slowly toward it.

The goons were nowhere in sight. I didn't see their head man either.

I lifted one side of the pot that was just above their car. It was very heavy, but slideable. I eased it back into place and removed Tonk's coke and bundle of marijuana and placed them between the flowers and the soil in the pot. Next, I took out my trusty Exacto and split the cocaine bag. I kept a pack of "Hits."

It's funny: As I prepared the dope for its permanent journey down, I felt a pang of reluctance, even though I never use the stuff. Such is the power of the media, always talking about its value. It didn't matter to me who used it, as long as the dope didn't use the person who was using it . . . ? Well, sometimes I don't make sense even to myself, but I knew what I meant. What mattered were the "preacher pushers," who tell you how *good* dope is. I hated them.

By methodically lifting one side of the pot, then the other, I slowly shoved it to the edge of the wall. I could have just pushed it off, but I wanted to make sure it landed on target. I checked the dope again and both packs seemed secure. I looked down to see where the thugs had gone but they were nowhere in sight. The pot teetered on the edge, positioned perfectly.

I let it fall.

It smashed right through the Aerostar's window, right where the driver would have been sitting, sheering off the steering wheel. The cocaine bag erupted from the force of the fall, spraying a fine white powder all over the front seats.

Unfortunately, I lingered a bit too long enjoying the view, and their tall, wiry leader looked up from across the street and spotted me. It was the same goon who caused me to drop my gyro—the S.O.B. He crossed purposefully and headed for the arcade.

As I turned to make my escape I saw two cops on horseback clopping down Pike Place. They hadn't spotted me because I was hidden from the sides by the remaining flower pots. The goon had been directly in front of me. The cops moved quickly toward the Aerostar. I nodded in satisfaction.

I made it to the door, opened it, bent down, removed the 7-Up can and tossed it in the garbage bin. Then I casually walked to the other door I had previously tested, opened it and made my exit.

Silently as possible, I made my way back to the street level. I knew I would be coming out directly by the damaged Aerostar, but I didn't worry because there were so many people milling about in the main arcade.

I was right; the crowd was so thick I could hardly open the door. Once out, I looked over and saw the cops questioning the two hoods who tried to nail me last night. Great! Their leader must have gone into Dunhill's looking for me.

I waited a moment as the cop peered into the car. I watched him wet his index finger, reach in and dab the driver's seat. When he pulled it out there was a bit of the white powder on it. He licked it, nodded to his partner, and moved to arrest the two goons. The pair looked as though they didn't know what hit them.

Flowerpot power!

I still had their boss to worry about, though, so I went up to the north arcade, reversed down the Pine Street corridor and into the second level, then reversed direction again and walked under the length of the main arcade. I crossed the little terrazzo at the entrance of the Ajax Hotel and went under the tunnel that entered Post Alley.

Bugsy's was just down from where I emerged, but I hesitated. I realized that the best place to hide out for awhile would be the most out-of-the-way place in the Market: the bar at Les Troyans!

I looked back up to the clock on the Corner Market Building. It read 10:30. I knew that at that time of the morning nobody would be up there. I climbed the narrow stairs that sprout out next to veggie stall number one.

The Market was rapidly filling up. I could barely make it across the plaza, and I had yet to work my way around Rachel. A TV crew was setting up to do some video work. Rachel was being ridden by about ten Japanese kids, who were arranging themselves for a photograph. Usually, as Fishmonger Emeritus, I would have had a boutonnière in my coat and volunteered to take a photo of the whole family. Today, I just slunk by.

I reassured myself that the goon couldn't possibly have followed me, so I stood a little straighter and smiled. I had recently learned that a big man with a frown on his face is very intimidating to average-size folks, and ever since I've tried to remember to smile. Of course, that's hard to do when you've just ruined a $20,000 car and sent two people up the river for a year or two. But, what the hey?

I detoured at the flower shop and bought a boutonnière—a pink carnation. The proprietress pinned it on my stained sweatshirt. It made me forget my nasty deed.

I tried to recall if I had ever done anything like that in my past, something so obviously malicious. I couldn't think of anything.

Well, I once threw a dummy out in front of a moving car when I was a kid. Wow, you should have seen the driver when he stopped; he was white as a sheet! Hmmm . . . Also, as a punk teenager, I laughed out the window at a funeral going by. Well, sure, I did a lot of kid-stuff pranks and shoplifting and such. Trying to prove how cool I was. But I never, ever . . .

Shit, I felt like a heel. What if those guys were just tourists and had no connection at all to Ricci? Another side of my brain kicked in and shouted down the guilt.

Focus!

I lifted my chin and gave a Look of Eagles. I proceeded past the 7C's Spice Shop and down the hallway to Les Troyans, into the little bar on the second floor.

I was wrong about the number of customers; it was almost full. The bar was very small, with room for four tables and five stools. It was connected to a banquet room that had a fantastic view of the Olympic Mountains on the horizon. A breakfast shindig was in progress, and three guests had spilled over to the bar for champagne cocktails: firm young ladies, whose rumps were squashed onto the flat-seated barstools.

I sat down at an unused table closest to the bar. To hell with the Olympics. I inched my seat over so that my head was less than one foot from the lasses' behinds. It was truly heaven.

When the bartender leaned between two of the young ladies and called for my order, they both turned and saw me smiling, looking up at them. They laughed and one of them patted my West Seattle Stetson.

I ordered a champagne cocktail, feeling like Toulouse-Lautrec.

As I turned back, I swear the girl wearing the red dress, the one on my right, pushed her thigh closer to me. Good God, almighty! Paul reared up like a divining rod hitting water. I gave my carnation to her.

The drink was handed to me between the girls, and I saluted the glass silently toward the west, saying, "To you, Dahlia, wherever you are." I took a sip and placed my glass on the table. Pulling out a fiver, I snaked my hand between the girls and paid for the drink.

When I turned around I was staring straight into the boss goon's eyes. He had stopped his climb two thirds of the way up the stairs. His eyes looked like the eyes of death twice warmed over. There was more white around his pupils than around a vanilla-covered donut, and his pupils were emptier than the donut's hole.

Paul dropped like a stone and a shiver ran up my spine. I tried to pull my eyes away from his, but it was no go. I was caught.

The goon slowly walked up the stairs, entered the bar and moved to my table. He didn't take a step, he just moved. One of the girls at the bar turned around, saw him, and quickly turned away. Through her skimpy blouse, I saw her backbone tense up.

He sat down at my table without asking and just looked at me. I was as nervous as a just-dead sardine on a hook and out of water. Kind of jerking like.

"Where is she?" he asked, his voice flat.

"I don't know what you're talking about," I replied, flabbergasted.

He asked again, his voice lowered to a guttural animal's growl.

"I don't care who you are or what you did to my car; I want to know where she is."

I was so scared I was ready to shit green nickels. I wanted to go to the bathroom in the worst way.

"Do you mind if I use the bathroom?" I asked, raising my hand stupidly, as though I were in a third-grade classroom.

Confusion registered on his face, and as he shifted in his seat I could see the shoulder holster beneath his coat. I hastily told him I'd be right back, got up, and grotesquely jerked past the bar into the bathroom. He followed.

I almost wet my pants as I unzipped. Trouble was, I could hardly pee with him standing behind me. Then he stuck the muzzle of the gun into my ribs and growled, "You're gonna pee right now because we're going for a nice long ride, pal." Though I couldn't remember whether I'd finished unzipping, I peed.

We returned to the cozy bar, with the gun wedged between us. The people in the bar sensed that something was up, but didn't quite understand. The gun was well concealed because the goon gripped my arm, holding me close.

We made it down the stairs and out into the hallway. He stopped right in front of one of the elevators that led down to Waterway, looking confused. I blurted out that the Aerostar was probably in the hands of the police by now and that I couldn't go for a ride.

He looked at me in the strangest way, then asked me which was the fastest way to the parking garage. I almost looked at the elevator, but checked myself and told him we would have to pass the big fish house and go down Flower Row. Again, I volunteered that the Aerostar was probably impounded by the cops.

"I don't know anything," I pleaded. "You've got the . . . the wrong person. That . . ." Suddenly, I just shut up. It was like at Dunhill's. A cool wave washed over me and I told him all right, I would tell him about Dahlia. He eyed me warily as I began walking.

"Not so fast." he said. "Slow down. We stay together or you're dead meat."

I became very cool. "You know, I've fallen in love with Ricci's girl."

He looked at me oddly.

I continued. "Yeah, she's been staying at my place. Great, great cover. You know, Ricci beat her. What's a class dude like that beating up on a frail, young homeless girl?"

The goon stared into the distance. A slight twitch invaded his tightly etched face.

"What's your name?" I asked.

He looked at me with his wide, evil eyes. "Sal," he grunted. "Go on. Keep talking."

"Well," I gulped, "all I can tell you is that I don't know where she is. Now. Uh, did you make love to her as well? She's pretty . . . young . . . firm legs. . . ? Hey, mind if I call you Salvadore?"

"Move," Sal grunted again, poking me in the side with his artillery. He was not amused at my attempt at cameraderie.

"Whatever you say, pal," I answered.

He shook like a dead, brittle tree in the middle of a windstorm and clenched my arm harder as we moved out into the main arcade. We were like Siamese twins, joined together by the muzzle of a snub-nosed pistol. I was sweating but I kept my cool. My thinking cap was on. Yes, now I understood. We were going to Tonk's truck. Tonk . . .

He was going to kill me.

I asked coolly, "Sal, what did you do with his body?"

"Whose body," he replied, a tight little smile on his face.

"Tonk. The street musician. You killed him."

"Oh him," he smirked. "Last time I saw him he was down in the dumps." He winked. "You know. Dumpster. You won't need visiting rights."

My alarm bells began ringing and my legs started to melt under me. I had to think fast.

We inched by a fish stall where the fishmongers were tossing the fish to the wrapper every time a customer placed an order. A throng of people were watching and taking snapshots. The act had become a famous TV spectacle, and nearly every celeb on TV has thrown a fish at some time or the other.

I noticed that one of the cameras was bigger than the others and bore the CNN logo on its side. I pointed to it. Sal looked and lost his concentration for a split second, long enough for me to slip in front of the live video camera.

Sal was as camera shy as he was cop shy. He grabbed my arm, but I shook him away. We both were now in front of the camera, and he pulled back.

I was free.

I stayed in front of the camera, walking sideways, smiling and waving. Paolo, one of the fishmongers, slapped my back with a haddock and told me to move on. The distance between me and Sal was growing, since he'd gotten swept up in the crowd behind the camera.

I made my move and dashed between the rows of fish and out in front of the Flower Row entrance. One thing about Flower Row— it hasn't seen flowers in thirty years. It's filled with colorful craft tables.

I came out of the fish stall in front of a leather goods maker and dashed across the small expanse, just as Sal broke free from the crowd.

I ducked down the steps that led to the public restroom, made a left, and entered a hallway leading to the mezzanine level. I passed the candy store and crossed the hall to the other side.

Chapter 12

Hercules Revisited

"Shoo-doo-be-doo, shoo-doo-be-doo de wah . . .
my loving baby . . ."

TALL, THIN SAL looked as mean as a shark fin as he sliced through the throngs of shoppers. I knew the Market's passage ways probably better than anyone, so I was safe at home. But did I want to be safe?

My brain worked overtime as I chose the same pathway through the Market I'd used two years earlier when running away from a cop who was trying to serve me with a stack of jaywalking tickets that had gone to warrant. Back then I disappeared like a ghost. This time I kept just thirty feet ahead of Sal as I tromped down Flower Row. Sal looked to be my senior by maybe ten years, but like his gangster buddies, was in far better shape than I would ever be.

I slipped into the Market's lower levels at the Mezzanine, then made a turn at the Pakistani silver shop, where Rubican, the owner, was speaking to his customers in a foreign tongue I took to be Pakistani. A short, narrow hallway took me past Valentino's Italian bulk food store, where the air was filled with scents of the Mediterranean. I paused at the end of the hall, just outside the Chinese gift shop, which was filled with Mandarins speaking in their melodic way. I was becoming quite disoriented, beginning to lose sight even of what country I was in. I was losing it. One half of me wanted to disappear, the other half didn't. I stood frozen at the end of the hall.

Sal appeared. He rushed toward me and I turned and entered the next shop. It's called Bolivio and features clothing from Bolivia. I saw the owner, Jim Tom, and self-consciously slipped through his thick displays of overflowing garment racks. Jim, who always wants to discuss Market politics, immediately headed in my direction. I brushed past him with a curt nod of my head. He saw my concern, and stopped to look behind me.

I moved on through the store, stopping at the other entrance, which faced a little balcony where one of the Market's two barbershops is located. I winked at Jane, a Market regular who was waiting for a haircut.

Jane is the Market's reigning sweetheart. She won the title in our annual ballot-stuffing contest last Valentine's Day. It's the only place in the city where voters are encouraged to stuff the ballot box for their favorite sweetheart.

I sensed that Sal had arrived and turned around. Jim yelled at him, but I didn't hear what he said. Jim put his foot out as Sal rushed by, and old Sal went sprawling in the middle of a rack of brightly colored peasant blouses. Sal was mad now, and he flung blouses in every direction, trying to regain his balance.

Jim began yelling at him to get out, pointing in the direction he'd come, but Sal focused on me, steadying himself against the balcony doorwell. I wondered what the hell I was leading him to. I didn't know why I was teasing him. Was I hoping that the next time he tripped he'd get seriously hurt and end up in the hospital?

Well, maybe.

I waited there until he righted himself. Meanwhile, Jane was coming out of the little barber shop toward me, her concern evident.

"Hey, what's wrong?" she yelled, moving in my direction.

I had to move quickly because she'd accidentally moved into Sal's path. Jane was tough, though, and she quickly sussed out the situation. She put some weight behind her elbow and slammed into Sal. Her blow only slowed him down, however, so I continued down the stairway, then ran for the second set of stairs that led to the third level. As Sal stumbled down the first stairway, I tucked out of sight under the stairs to catch my breath.

The sudden movement on the balcony had thrown my back out, and I stood there momentarily, wincing in middle-aged pain. I was getting worried, wondering what in the hell I was going to do next. Then I spotted the entrance to Hercules' studio. As I stared at his "Hercules, the Fortune Teller," sign, the smaller sign below listing his hours of business, and the sliding sign that read "unoccupied," a plan began to formulate

I was hidden behind a latticed kiosk that people used to staple announcements on. Through the maze of posters and scraps of paper I kept tabs on Sal. He'd stopped at the base of the stairs and was just standing there, his arms stiffly at his sides like some sort of penguin. Then he crouched down and moved from side to side, looking for me. There were no customers on this level at the moment, and I realized that any motion would give me away.

As I watched him, he nonchalantly pulled a cobbler's hammer out from under his jacket, tapped it twice in his palm, and slipped it into an outside pocket.

That did it! Once was enough. Suddenly my back pain disappeared. Coolly, I took out my felt tipped pen and uncorked it, keeping it at the ready as I crept alongside the kiosk closest to Hercules' door. Sal was barely twenty feet away on the other side of the stairs, hidden by the kiosk under the stairwell.

I inched forward in a stooped position because the damn kiosk was only about five feet high, and he might have a clear shot at my other ear if I stood straight up. Fortunately, he'd moved over to the center of the hallway and was looking north, toward MacPherson's. I had just a few seconds to act before he turned my way.

I shuttled across to Hercules' entrance, which was barely out of Sal's line of vision. When I reached the door, I quickly crossed out Hercules' name and inscribed "Ken" over it. The sign now read "Ken, the Fortuneteller." I recorked the pen and returned to the relative safety of the kiosk. I peeked around the opposite end.

Sal saw me instantly and began moving toward me. I turned and ran for Hercules' door, opened it and rushed in, shutting it immediately.

The room was dimly lit. A spotlight focused on Hercules, dressed in his Barbie Dolls, and sitting on his throne that was decorated with the dollhouse furniture. He was reading *The Wall Street Journal* with a penlight.

He saw me and turned off the light. A smile of recognition started to form on his lips. I left a breathless "Hi . . ." unfinished and dangling on the air as I moved rapidly past his dais toward the studio's side exit. I opened the door quickly, finishing my salute to Herc with a resounding ". . . KEN!" As I slipped into the narrow side hallway, I caught a glimpse of Herc's eyes shifting from warmth to rage.

I leaned heavily on the exit door, feeling half guilty for what I'd just unleashed. I justified to myself that I had to do something to stop the chase before someone, other than Sal, got hurt. I breathed slowly to catch my breath. The pain in my neck returned as I heard the fortune teller's door being opened by Sal. It had to have been a newcomer like Sal, because the next thing I heard was a deep Brooklyn voice.

"Ken?"

It seemed as though ages went by during that tense silence behind the door. I counted under my breath, "Ken one-thousand, Ken two-thousand . . ." Right after I reached three I heard Sal's loud, deep questioning call.

"Ken?" it repeated, more loudly.

What I heard next was the clatter of what I presumed was the dreaded hammer hitting the floor, followed by a sound like a gurgling fire hydrant being crushed by a cement truck. I assumed that was the last sound that would ever come from Sal's Brooklyn-bred foul mouth.

I thanked the stars and the gods that Sal hadn't thumped Herc.

I wiped the sweat from my forehead, took a deep breath, and moved out from the side hallway. I looked once over at Hercules' front door, then turned back into the main hallway like a man who'd just finished a ripe Sunset and Alvarado burrito. It felt so good going down, but man, my stomach did ache.

I continued out of the lower level by the Pine Street corridor, the way that Sal correctly guessed I would have gone. As I passed MacPherson's, a fine old English-style hotdog joint, I felt that old primordial tug at my synapses strumming me directly into the place.

To hell with focus.

MacPherson's is the only place in the city I know of where you can get a tasty soft ice cream cone made with real cream. I always say that there is no addiction in the world like the one to mother's milk, so I ordered two cones. A young girl took my two dollars, gave me change, and off I walked with a cone in each hand.

"Best way to settle the nerves," I told myself as I took a wicked lick at the cone in my left hand. In any case, they were a just reward for a job well done. I told myself that, after some time had passed, I'd tell Hercules what I'd done. I knew he would just smile. He's above guilt and other mortal things like that.

At the stairwell just beyond MacPherson's, I decided not to go up to the main arcade and instead headed down to Waterway Avenue to sit under the Thinking Piece, as I call it, which is a kind of angled obelisk sculpture.

As I glanced down at it I found myself thinking, "Just like me—

slightly askew." I smiled at the thought, and accepted the word for the first time. It sounded better than weird, or crazy or just plain nuts. "Askew," I thought. Maybe I was passing through some sort of cultural barrier. No more being a weirdo; no more a nutso; just "slightly askew."

I made it to the obelisk and sat on its wide base, finishing the first cone. The second one had begun to drip, so I had to take nips at it from time to time.

The obelisk is located at the base of the stairs. At the foot of the stairwell runs by dreaded Waterway Avenue. Across from where I sat was a weed-strewn vacant lot, partially used as a parking lot. The Market buildings that had once stood on the lot had been destroyed over twenty years ago in the name of urban renewal.

At one of those endless Market meetings, I'd learned that the lot had been part of the Market back then, but had never been built upon because of developer competition for the site. Through the years these "developo-parasites," coveting but not understanding the Market's success, have periodically waved fancy development plans at city officials. But the community has always fought them off.

The problem is, the developers never think of the actual welfare of the Market, and their plans call for super highrises that would rob the Market of its views. The last developer was stopped because the community threatened to sue for the value of the views. Market traditionalists learned about the value of the views by studying a building with a similar view which had been built a few blocks north of the Market. In that case, the builders had been required to cut out a whole section of the building to preserve the view of a powerful corporation whose headquarters were just behind the new building. When streetwise Market folks calculated what it cost the developer to carve away half his building, the figure was in the tens of millions. When a lawyer who loved the Market waved this fact in front of city hall—Bam!—the development was stopped.

Trouble is, the Market's powers-to-be have never developed a Market-related plan for the site. So it sits, underutilized, a freeway to hell. I say freeway to hell because, just beyond the site is a double-decker highway viaduct, slicing Seattle's waterfront away from the rest of the city. And under the viaduct is what's called "the Jungle." Seattle's untouchables live there, the case-hardened homeless.

As I sat there under the obelisk, I watched some hooded rag pickers slowly pushing the infested, junk-filled shopping carts they'd glommed from a supermarket somewhere. With their hooded and drooped heads they were like slow-motion, earthbound vultures, coming from hell, from the Jungle, a place I don't even want to think about. Hooded creatures, weaving out to fan the city, looking for discarded stuff. Some are called "beefeaters" because they supposedly eat human flesh.

I looked down into the wastes, thinking that even the cops don't go there. A while ago, I heard one comment to a bunch of people at a bar that "the bums are in the weeds now." When a self-righteous sort said "They shouldn't have to be down there," the cop yelled, "Where the hell else do you want them to be, back on the street again?"

Over the years I have seen many street people make the streets their permanent home. They have to, since constant lack of nutrition destroys their health to the point where they're worse than zombies.

I knew that Herc wasn't a zombie, but I knew he visited the Jungle from time to time. Who was going to stop him? Years ago, when they couldn't find the person he was suspected of killing, many thought the body had ended up in the communal soup kitchen in the center of the Jungle.

That was the last time the police made a raid. Later, they claimed they had found nothing human in the soup, though they had found a large mound of finely crunched bone next to it. Analysis showed that it was boiled bones and teeth from many sources, including dogs and cats. It was rumored that human bones had also been found, but no one was talking. There was nothing to connect Herc to the scene, so he hadn't been charged with anything, but I had a hunch that the Jungle was where Herc would take Sal's body to dispose of—his way.

I remembered when Herc was in the California jail system. It was after he had gone completely within himself after the Venetian dope thing twenty years ago. A short time after that he exploded and badly beat up two men named Ken in Santa Monica. That got him a year in jail. But he was so quiet and well-mannered he ended up working on a road crew for the County of Los Angeles. The authorities discovered that once he started using a sledge hammer, he entered into a zone of sorts. He could spend hours smashing stone with his sledge.

I saw him from my car once in Van Nuys. You couldn't miss him because he was so big. His crew was tearing up a street, presumably to lay some power lines or fix a water pipe. I was transfixed by his methodical use of his sledge, pounding the stone into a fine powder.

Yes, I knew that Herc visited the Jungle, but I didn't volunteer the information about his past to the investigators.

Chapter 13

Deacon's Past

"Early times, early times . . . make my feet all right . . ."

FOR QUITE A WHILE I just sat there, thinking about Herc and the old days. My mind drifted to Montecito, home, Grandpa Dave Davenport Shasta the first, Papa James Davenport the second, and me, Deacon Davenport, with my third name I never used—Shasta.

When I was growing up, the kids ribbed me about a lot of things. The biggest ribbing was over my name. My true friends called me Dave, short for Davenport. But the ribbers called me "Inport" sometimes and "Outport" other times, depending on their moods. As a joke they would ask me if I was related to Mount Shasta. Or demand that I pay them for used Shasta cola bottles. It pissed me off no end. Eventually it was "Deek the Geek, Deek the Geek, Deek the Geek!" over and over, because I had to become a clown to survive. The "Geek" moniker stuck with me over the years.

In the late Forties, when I was six or seven, Grandpa lost all his money in a bad business deal. Unfortunately, Montecito was a rich person's town, and we were decidedly not rich after that. My mother left to live with a would-be film star and completely forgot about us.

So Pop and I lived with his parents. Grandpa's big house went to seed because, even though Pop had a good job, it wasn't nearly enough to keep the huge house going. Grandpa lost his health in the early Fifties, but still took me down to the Santa Barbara pier to gab with the fishermen. We even fished a bit.

Grandma and he would also take me to the Farmer's Market on Fairfax in Los Angeles. I loved it down there. While Grandma went shopping and Grandpa played dominos with his friends, I took off and got lost among all the produce stands.

My old man worked at Douglas Aircraft in Culver City. His favorite spot was POP—Pacific Ocean Park amusement park—and the Santa Monica pier carney area.

I remember him having to go to Seattle to deal with Boeing, Douglas's biggest competitor in the airplane business. He hated Boeing because it was growing, and—I suspect—he thought it was a threat to his job. He would come back from Seattle mad as hell. He always drank, but started drinking heavily in the mid-Fifties. He started in the old from-sugar-to-shucks-to-shit routine. He didn't quite make it to the shit phase.

At that time, the only roadworthy car in our family was Pop's '57 Chevy coupe. Grandpa's big green Bugatti hadn't been running for over ten years because engine parts were so expensive. Then Pop totaled the Chevy and installed its big 327 engine in Grandpa's car. Trouble was, the Bugatti had old-fashioned metal brakes, and when Pop first tried the car on the road, he gunned it to up over a hundred, had to stop suddenly, and the brakes failed. Pop died in the crash. The cops said he was drunk at the time.

I joined the Navy at seventeen and did my duty at Kwajelin in the South Pacific. While I was in the Navy Grandma died. Shortly thereafter Grandpa lost the house to the county for not paying his taxes, and ended up in an old folks' home on the money from the tax sale. He died three months after entering the home. I couldn't attend the funerals because the Navy wouldn' grant special consideration leave. Grandfolks weren't considered part of your immediate family.

So, with all my relatives gone, when I left the Navy in San Diego I had no place to go and in a month I'd gone through the few hundred I'd saved. I ended up broke on the beach in Venice, not far from POP. I got a job there as a high-striker, handing out mallets to people so they could take smacks at trying to ring a bell on a tall pole.

Then Smokey entered my life, and that led to my Hollywood career. Smokey was about ten years older—bullshit, twenty years older—and a hundred years wiser. We became lovers. She worked in the movies and taught me a lot about life. What to wear and all that. I had known all this as a young man, but had been rapidly losing touch as I was struggling simply to survive. Then I became a model for a catalogue agency and got to keep the clothes they fitted for me because I had such a unique torso. Big chest and stubby legs. Today my torso just kind of flows together.

Well, that was one of the high points of my Hollywood career.

I looked down at my belly, then at my knee caps peeking out. No legs. Man, did I feel stout!

Focus!

I took a deep breath and pulled out of my reminiscing. I was beginning to feel hungry. I decided to take a ride over to West Seattle and eat at the Luna.

I got up from my perch by the obelisk a little too quickly and almost fell over because my legs had fallen asleep. I shook them while holding on to the ledge. I exaggerated a bit by kicking my legs high in the air, like a stubby can-can dancer, for the benefit of people passing by in their cars. I got three beeps.

Once the buzzing in my legs stopped, I made my way down Waterway. I looked in at Bradley's Reptile House and the thoughts I'd been suppressing resurfaced. I had to teach Ricci a lesson before he and Dahlia left the city. How I was going to do it wasn't clear yet.

I stopped at the old phone booth by the steps leading up to the Market and pondered. I pulled out its filthy phone book and found the number for The Grand Hotel. I dropped the book and thought about dialing but stopped.

I had to plan how I was to surprise him. Perhaps I could use my girth to my advantage. I certainly needed to find some advantage, because Ricci looked wire tough and probably had killed before—and not only women. I hadn't killed so much as a fly. Well, that wasn't quite true anymore; I had helped kill Sal.

A pang of guilt penetrated my girth. I fought the feeling, clenching my fists. One side of my dumb brain was saying yes, the other side a resounding no.

Okay, I thought, a man died. But odds are he killed Tonk. How many lives had Herc and I saved? Sal was in the business of killing. *Focus!*

I entered the elevator that led up to the front door of Les Troyans. It was the elevator I had almost told Sal about barely an hour before. Boy, was I glad I hadn't.

I got off on the floor below "the Troy" and entered a little patio that the Ajax Hotel lobby fronted. I went around the hotel and took the passageway that led into Post Alley. It was the same path I'd taken to avoid Sal.

Hmmm. I knew now how he'd found me. Just like anybody would, we both went to the center of the Market, consciously or unconsciously: "Meet me at the Pig!"

I turned into the alley, avoiding Bugsy's. I had no reason to check in. I wanted to leave the Market and do some thinking.

I unlocked my red scoot, squeezed my helmet on and putt-putted down the alley, making my way to the waterfront. The sea air was crisp and warmed by the afternoon sun.

I scooted south past the huge freighter I'd seen last night from

Bugsy's. Several cranes were unloading it. They looked like a flock of spindly dinosaurs, glinting in the blue sky.

I turned at the Spokane Street "mess" as I called it. The level of air pollution was comparable to Wilmington below L.A. A blizzard of belching trucks in a desert of concrete. Not a green tree in sight. My lungs froze up in disgust as I traveled across Harbor Island and up the Duwamish Bridge. I got a slight headache and remembered why I never came to this part of town. I made it past the huge steel mill and under a pile of concrete spaghetti that fed the freeways high over my head.

On the other side I entered another of my worlds—the Luna Cafe. It was on Avalon Way and surrounded by trees and lush gardens full of rhododendrons and geraniums. I parked the scoot out front and went inside.

The cafe was a repository of old signs, antiques and amusement games from the days of the Luna Park Amusement Park. It had been torn down in the Twenties, so I'd never seen it, but I imagined that it resembled Pacific Ocean Park in Santa Monica.

I ordered a hamburger and studied the miniature jukebox on the table before punching in three tunes for a quarter. Ditties from the Fifties: "Jambalaya" by Hank Williams, "Nature Boy" by Nat King Cole, and "So Fine" by the Chiffons.

As old Hank started to wail, my mind reared up and yelled "Focus!" The word roared through my synapses, snapping them to attention. I had to plan how I was going to approach Ricci.

I used the pay phone on the wall by the door to call The Grand Hotel. The number had burned itself in my memory when I had looked it up on Waterway Avenue. Before the phone began to ring, I changed my mind, hung up, and dialed the *Exacto* first. I let the phone ring three times, then hung up just before the answering machine kicked in on the fourth ring. How I hated "Yankee Doodle Dandy." I used the same quarter to phone The Grand.

The operator answered and I asked for Mr. Solano. Again she told me that he had left word not to be disturbed. I hung up without saying another word.

I looked at the "Call for Philip Morris" clock on the wall. It was 12:30.

I returned to my booth, totally perplexed. Across from me was a Buddy Holly poster.

I started humming, "The day the music died."

What the hell was I going to do next? Go to The Grand and confront him? What do cops do? What do robbers do?

"Can't do nothing until something happens." That's what a blues song told me a while back.

I took out my pen and looked for some paper. Put your problems down on paper, then work it out, that's what Grandpa would say.

The only paper I had with me was the folded back side of the Market Design and Review Committee announcement. I unfolded it and read the agenda.

It was weird. I felt that it was a very important document. It seemed so familiar. I remembered that I had concentrated on it when the goon was coming toward me down Post Alley. It said that the meeting was set for one o'clock. The clock on the wall read 12:45. A brilliant white light went on in my scrambled brains. My synapses were strumming in unison.

The hamburger arrived. I took one bite, put it down, dropped a fiver on the table and headed out.

It must have been the first time I never finished a burger. Grandma would certainly not have approved.

Chapter 14

The Chicken Stand

"No windows, no doors, just a hole in the wall;
yeah, the chicken shack . . ."

I SHOWED UP at the Design and Review Committee meeting half an hour before the allotted time for the review of Ramona Bianca's chicken stand. The three committee members present had arranged themselves on one side of the wide table in the manager's conference room. They were well-meaning, but they sure were haughty in their imperious role of "yea" or "nay" over a person's proposed livelihood.

The hopefuls, with their supporters, sat in huddled groups on the other side of the table. Ramona was in the back, wearing black on black, the perfect image of an Italian peasant woman. Next to her was a tall, elegant man, with a white mane of hair flowing beyond his collar. Perhaps about sixty and, I would imagine, a two-hundred-dollar-an-hour-plus attorney. I know I was being presumptuous, but still. They paid me no mind because they were intent on the proceedings.

Señor Mane, as I thought of him, was taking notes on everything. Ramona, by his side, listened intently to the proceedings. Every once in awhile they huddled together as he pointed out his observations.

I noticed the scribblings on the agenda of the person sitting next to me. According to his jottings, so far the Design and Review Committee had not recommended any of the applicants. The one presently being considered was the ceramist. She was blonde, tall and willowy. I sussed her out as a weekend artist from the suburbs, bored with her life and attempting to change it. Her art was adequate, but that didn't matter to the committee. They were worried about her commitment to her business.

I looked at her plans; they were not well thought out. But then, the Market is supposed to be an incubator for new businesses, so she should have the right of others before her. That meant she had the right to learn retail the hard way, right from the very bottom of the learning curve.

By this time the arguments were over and a vote was asked for. Sure enough, they advised against her. Judging from the reaction of the willowy one, it was the first time in her life she had been denied anything. She looked at the committee with such disbelief that the chair told her that if she wanted to rethink her plans, she was welcome to re-present her project. The chair also, in an offhand way, said she could present her case directly to the Historic Commission at the next day's meeting, since the committee had just an advisory role. He quickly added, though, that the Historic Commission would probably go along with the Design and Review Committee's recommendations.

She left in a real huff, ignoring the sign-up sheet just outside the door for the next day's Historic Commission meeting agenda.

The fried chicken shop was next on the docket. Ramona and Señor Mane came forward to sit in the chairs that had just been vacated.

The contrast between the two was apparent to all, especially the committee members. She was short and stocky and dressed in black; he was the very picture of fashion in his three-piece tailored suit. When she spoke, she had a thick, Southern Italian dialect; one could almost hear the Sicilian guttural sounds she must have spent years trying to eliminate. He, on the other hand, sounded very Manhattan as he introduced himself as Mr. Sands, "the attorney for Mrs. Ramona Bianca."

They both bowed slowly to the committee members, who responded by nodding in unison. Señor Mane—Sands—rolled out the expensive overlays that some designer must have charged thousands of dollars to produce. The committee members studied them, duly impressed, then asked who the designer was. Ramona looked confused until Sands bent over to coach her.

"A member of the family," she said in firm but broken English.

When asked how many members were in her family, she consulted with the Mane again.

"Fifteen," she answered.

The board was impressed, but smelled a way of defeating this peasant of a woman who had dared to approach them with such a professional business plan. She was asked if the fried chicken shop was a family effort.

Ramona was now into the spirit of the inquiry. Yes, she nodded.

Again, she was asked how many sons and daughters she had.

"Three sons, two daughters."

"Will they be working at the store?"

"Yes."

"What about your husband?"

"Dead."

"With you, your daughters and sons, that only makes six people. Who are the other nine?"

This threw Ramona, so Sands bent over again to coach her.

"My brothers and sisters, and their sons and daughters," she said, recovering.

This stumped the committee into a moment's silence. Then the most tart-tongued committee member asked Ramona who was funding the stand.

Once again Sands advised her, and she replied that the whole family had put their money together for the stand.

Miss Tart asked the final question.

"You're going to run the chicken stand?"

"Yes."

There was complete silence for about ten seconds. Then the committee asked for public testimony.

Kim, the Korean owner of the Chicken Town stand in the main arcade, screamed as she always did when potential competition might be allowed in the Market. She had screamed the previous year when Alex's Free Roamin' Inn concept had been approved over her arguments. Alex, who had asked me to show up at the meeting, argued next against Ramona starting the business, saying that the Market was saturated with chicken stands.

I smiled to myself. The Market has easily eight or ten million visitors a year; there was room for several more chicken stands.

Kim walked over to the table and picked up Ramona's plans. She was about to dump them in the waste can but Ramona grabbed them from her.

Kim howled that it would take a million dollars to build her stand. She pointed at Ramona and asked, "Does she look like a woman who has a million dollars?"

Again there was a pregnant silence, and the chair quickly said, "If there isn't anyone else who wants to speak. . . ?"

Alex looked directly at me; I shook my head no.

The chair spoke: "May I remind the committee that business competition is not one of our concerns. And in saying that, I ask that we vote."

They took a vote, and for no good reason but haughtiness, rejected Ramona's application.

I thought to myself that I would have spoken in favor of the application. It was a sound one, regardless of where the money for funding it was coming from. The hint was in Ramona's constant use of the term "family."

Then it came to me in a rush: Ricci was the money guy. More accurately, he was sent here by the Mafia—okay, the "extended family"—to set up Ramona's fried chicken operation. What a perfect scenario. The Market is the number-one people place in the country. Many, many businesses are started here, such as Seattle's famous coffee companies.

I followed Bianca and Sands and stopped them before they left the building. I pointed out to them that if they wanted a chance to realize their business plan, then they had to sign up for tomorrow's Historic Commission meeting. I pointed to the sign-up sheet by the window of the conference room. The committee eyed me warily. They realized I knew that the full commission could very well allow a business to be created against their recommendations.

I explained that I would help them. Sands and Bianca looked at each other questioningly, then turned to me. Like a true New Yorker, Sands asked almost exactly the same question that Sal had asked at his Aerostar.

"Why would you, a total stranger, want to help us?"

I explained a bit about who I was and my new objective of keeping Market traditions alive, including helping new businesses like theirs get started. Ramona looked at me astutely and made the internationally understood cupped-hand, palm-up gesture.

"Two thousand dollars," I replied.

Ramona gasped and lapsed into indecipherable Italian as Sands scratched his head. I shrugged my shoulders and pointed out how much money they must have already put out for the plans.

"Two grand is nothing. You people know that. I want a thousand up front, and another thousand immediately after approval is given. Have your backer bring the money to Bugsy's Pizzeria at six o'clock."

I looked at my watch. "That's in two hours"

I uncorked my felt-tip pen, took the plans folder from Ramona, and drew a map with directions to Bugsy's.

"Have him park here on Waterway Avenue. Climb the Hillclimb. It will be marked, "Hillclimb." Then cross the patio under where we're standing." I gestured with my fingers. "Straight through the Ajax Hotel Lobby. Bugsy's is at the end of the hall. 'Ajax" is spelled A-J-A-X.

"Just the backer," I stressed. "Neither one of you should come. If I'm seen with either of you before the meeting, it will look like the fix is on. Got me?"

They started wrangling, Italian style, but I curtly shut them up with more instructions. "Either the person representing your interests comes alone tonight, or it's no deal!"

"You're cheap; you're damn cheap," Sands blurted.

I ignored the insult. "By the way, sir," I said, "don't wear such expensive looking clothes tomorrow; dress down."

I walked away, leaving them standing there looking after me.

As soon as I was out of sight, I rushed over to the Market Information Booth and watched them through a rack of free newspapers and brochures.

Sands had taken out his cellular phone and was talking into it. Ramona was standing angrily with her arms folded, peasant style, over her plump tummy. I knew that my bait had been taken when Sands hung up and they returned to the conference room to register for the next day's meeting.

At least *someone* can get through The Grand's phone people, I thought.

I checked my pocket watch and saw that I had barely two hours to prepare for my meeting with their money man. I prayed I was right and that it was Ricci. It had to be Ricci; nothing else made any sense.

I made my way to the Benign Plumb coffee bar, which is tucked in an out-of-the-way area. I ordered coffee and began to arrange my thoughts.

I began with my usual prelude.

"Focus!" I said aloud.

Two customers overheard me and looked at me questioningly. I ignored them and concentrated on the scenario that was unfolding. I was no longer just an observer, I was becoming a participant. No, now I was the main man!

I knew now that Ricci held but one last puzzle piece. Unfortunately for me it was the major one: Dahlia. But I had most of the pieces in place now. A picture was forming. The negative space had been filled in.

Hmmm, I thought, Salvadore's disappearance is going to give Ricci something to think about, give HIM a frame to fill. If I just keep daubing with the brush, he'll get the picture soon enough. I just have to help him paint it.

Focus!

When I felt enough time had elapsed, I returned to the Market's main arcade. There, crowds were swirling, cash registers were ringing, and hawkers were yelling out various seafood specials. The bustling majesty of a market humming in top gear gave no hint of the weird drama taking place along her endless passageways.

I used the elevator that serviced the Ajax Hotel and returned to Waterway Avenue, six flights below. I stepped out and assessed the bleakness of the street.

"Car Window Row" some call it, because it's basically empty at night except for the odd parked car. Contingents of on-the-edge folks survive by smashing the car windows of country hicks dumb enough to park there at night.

Lights along Waterway are important because they make this element of society think twice about ransacking a car—or doing a mugging, for that matter. I walked up to the phone booth in the pocket-size parking lot where I had looked up The Grand's telephone number and used the foul-smelling phone book a second time, this time to smash the booth light.

I hummed an impromptu blues riff as I reentered the nearby elevator.

"If all goes right, there'll be a mugging tonight. . . ."

I rode up to the fifth floor and the entrance to the Ajax. I checked off the instructions to Ramona and Sands that I'd jotted down on the back of her plans. I looked over my shoulder at the route up from Waterway Avenue via the Hillclimb. I was satisfied I had it just right. I thought of putting up an arrow, giving directions to Bugsy's, because that part of the pathway was a bit obscure. Then, again. . . .

I went inside the Ajax foyer and found a stack of flyers advertising dates that the Market's rummage sales were to be held. The flyer was quite detailed for, like everything in the Market, this had become a popular daily event. It's the only rummage sale in the city where pro pickers aren't given first pickings, so it was understood that truly rare treasures could be found there. Like my antique brass floor ashtray, for instance, which had been painted a dumb shade of pink that disguised the brass and its real value.

Paid five bucks and have a standing offer of a hundred and thirty bucks if I ever want to sell it.

"Yahoo!" I hollered, aloud.

I looked around quickly to make sure no one had heard my joyous outburst.

Focus, I reminded myself, focus!

I shrugged my shoulders, brought out my felt-tip and wrote: "Bugsy's—this way," and drew an arrow beneath. I found some Scotch tape, zipped off a length, went over to the window and taped it where Ricci would see it.

I went out to the hallway to admire my handiwork. As I capped the felt-tip, I thought how much this whole sad caper was like a comic book plot. I walked down the hall and entered Bugsy's. There were a few customers inside so I set up my screen.

I took out my Canon bubblejet typewriter and plugged it in. My photocopied library file on Ricci Solano was lying on top of the small filing cabinet. I opened it and began re-reading the newspaper clippings.

I pulled out the *New York Times* Blind had sold me two days ago. I noticed the date and thought that, with luck, Blind was just at the beginning of his drinking cycle.

I looked out on the gathering gloom forming along Waterway. The street's bulky, purposeful six-story brick buildings, which had served as produce commission houses at the turn of the century, were in heavy shadow. The sun went down early there.

I wondered if I should have directed Ricci to park there. What if he was mugged when he got out of his car? What if Dahlia was with him and would wait until he returned from our meeting?

I rethought my plans. There was still time to call the thing off. Just phone The Grand and announce: "You don't know me, but we're meeting tonight to decide the fate of your company's—the Mafia, ha, ha, ha!—multimillion dollar efforts to establish a chain of fried chicken shops, and I told your people I could help you create the prototype shop right here in the epicenter of grassroots capitalism, U.S.A. Well, it was all a joke. Yes, Ricci, Mr. Solano. Sorry, chum, it was all a trick to get to you. Harm intended. By the way, if you're afraid, you could park up where it's safe and leave Dahlia at the hotel, okay? By the way, could I talk to her?"

I was just about to play the role of Ricci when the arriving ferry's toot brought me back to the task at hand. I shuddered involuntarily, feeling that old primordial fear of death. I could have kicked myself for being a gutless worrywart.

Well, a part of me is, I thought.

The negative crap lasted barely a second before a powerful feeling welled up in me, forcing me to focus. I felt like Job or Hamlet or Elvis looking at a burger: "To eat or not to eat?" Well, I didn't want to end up like Job, Hamlet or Elvis, so I dug in.

I arranged newspaper clippings around the photo of Ricci in the *New York Times,* then set up the Canon and composed a headline. This wasn't as easy as it sounds, and it took many attempts before I was satisfied with the result. When I finally printed it out, it read: *"Ricci Solano Indicted for the Murder of Esther Lents in Miami."* The subhead read, *"Year-long secret investigation by city attorneys leads to indictment."*

I taped my creation down, closed my office, and went upstairs to the Market's management offices. There was another meeting in progress, and the ever-present Garfield was at it again, seated among his supporters, waving a handful of notes in wide arcs. Heads bobbed out of the way as he made his point with broad gestures. All eyes were on his performance. I really admired his commitment to the community, but I also wished he would focus.

Ah, that great word: "Focus."

I turned back to the job at hand, and had no more interruptions as I used the photocopy machine to duplicate my phony cover. The size was a limitation, but with a heavy felt-tipped black border drawn around the picture I could hide the telltale line of the pasted-on dummy. When I got it just right, I folded the altered front page around the rest of the paper. Since I had never read it in the first place, it looked like a brand new paper.

As I admired my efforts, I thought that even if Ricci discovered it was a hoax, it would give him plenty to worry about.

I went up and across Pike Place to the rummage hall. The rummage people were packing up for the day so I had to hurry. I found two boxes of old tapes and searched till I found a Vivaldi. I smiled and paid my two bits. You can find anything you want at the Market if you know where to look.

I returned to Post Alley with the Vivaldi and my phony *New York Times* to give to Blind Spaghetti, but he hadn't arrived yet.

I glanced at my watch nervously. Where is Blind when you need him, I wondered.

I went back inside Bugsy's, ordered a TK from Nan, the new waitress, and asked her to play the Vivaldi later when I gave her the nod. She was getting ready for the dinner crowd and was in a bit of a hurry. She took one look at me and sneered. I explained that it was a very special dinner. She said okay and served me as if I were dead meat.

I took my beer over to my seat and looked down on Waterway. Cars were leaving for the night, and plenty of spaces were available. I figured that the Lamborghini had less than an hour if it was to survive in one piece. I didn't think there would be a problem since our meeting shouldn't take more than twenty, maybe thirty minutes.

A few minutes later I'd be mugging him in the phone booth.

I reminded myself that I was not mugging him for money. I just wanted to beat him within an inch of his life so he'd know that Dahlia had a guardian angel and that he'd better take care of her from now on. I also wanted to get in a few hits for Tonk.

Poor Tonk. I had to do something for him. Get his truck and store it at Dutch's lot.

My thoughts carried me back to Dahlia. Where was she? I suddenly remembered that my first love ever was named Dahlia.

Or was it Rose?

It was in Cambria, when I was about twelve.

Or was it Marigold?

We had had a picnic in the sand dunes.

Where was Dahlia, Rose, Marigold—whatever her name was—now, I wondered. Probably a suburban housewife with six kids. A grandmother, perhaps. Maybe she was Dahlia's mother.

I smiled at the thought of my bouquet having a teenage lover. A young man who took off from an inbred family living deep inside the Arctic Circle. But then I realized that wouldn't have happened.

The boy would have responsibilities at a very young age.

But a girl. Dahlia. What were her responsibilities? What forces shaped her personality? Keeping her and others warm? Bundling? That leads to sex, that most primal of pleasures which ensures the survival of the species in one of the harshest environments on earth.

Made sense to me. Made a lot of sense because Dahlia was so wise, yet so vulnerable. The perfect victim for a Ricci.

I wondered where she was being held. Most likely at The Grand, a captive of back-handed luxury. I grimaced.

When I first met her she had been wearing just a green skirt and halter. Nothing else. Well, her underwear. He must have bought her a snazzy wardrobe, so at least she had clothes.

The goons. Would they have taken her?

No, she must be with Ricci.

If Tonk was killed by the goons, what was the motive? To silence him? Had he panicked and become uncontrollable?

I shook my head, my logic line broken. I was sure of just one thing: If anything could save Dahlia, it would be the lust factor fueling Ricci. Mighty powerful juice, that combination. She lives or dies by her manipulation of his lust.

I tried once again to piece it all together. Okay, the goons and Sal were in town to keep Ricci in line until the fried chicken stand deal was approved. That's it. Salvadore was sent here to watch over Ricci, to see that he didn't get involved with women, to make sure he didn't embarrass the Mafia. Or should I say "the Family?" They found out about Dahlia, and Sal and Company came running.

I affected a Brooklynese grunt: "Just do the job, Ricci. No complications."

Hmmm.

If this theory was right, what effect would Salvadore's disappearance have on Ricci? It would make him feel unsure of himself, right? Yes! He would be concerned.

Then a thought came to me. Ricci's father had recently died. He had been a most respected member of the hierarchy. If the news clippings were accurate, then there would be many in the Family who would want Ricci to pay for his father's death.

Georgio Solano represented a potential future, a respectable future for the Mafia. His son represented the cruel past.

Focus!

Hard to figure all the angles. One thing for certain, I thought, Salvadore is dead. So let's see: Ricci found Dahlia, so now I'm going to send him a message.

The puzzle was complete.

I had to face it: I would be no match for Ricci in an even fight. But in the confines of a phone booth. . . ?

Moth to light, moth to light.

I had to give Ricci the message.

I recalled Ted's advice: Love is an obsession to rise above. Damn! Ted: the mind of a master logician. A fine mind like Mr. Spock's, a father figure with big ears. Well, Ted doesn't have the big ears. The oversized orifice connected to his brain is his mouth.

A cookie or cup of coffee will start Ted narrating in detail a 1930s radio show, a Shakespearean sonnet, a blues riff, a TV show like episode thirty-three of *I Love Lucy*. He'll tell you the complete plot and review it as he goes along. I've learned to just give in and listen, for buried in his recitations are many kernels of wisdom. It's just that getting at them takes the patience of a genius jazz conductor like Duke Ellington. Duke, who stayed on the track of his compositions, but allowed his soloists to improv to greatness.

With Ted, I can initiate a conversation by creating a "what if" situation around a genuine problem. Nine times out of ten Ted comes up with an old theatrical story that's his way of relating a parable of wisdom. I've always believed that true wisdom can be explained in five words or less, but in Ted's case I've had to throw that rule out the window—and fast.

Damn, I wish Ted was here.

The ferry in the harbor tooted its departure horn, and the blast jolted me out of my mental retardations. I laughed and reassured myself that Ted's old shows were created for an audience, so they rarely resembled actual life experiences. But, invariably, his telling them got me to thinking and helped me form a course of action.

Well, I'm on my own on this one, I thought.

I checked my watch again, then stared up at the two clocks on the wall. One told the time in Seattle, the other one gave the time in Chicago.

Kind of fun.

Chapter 15

Rendezvous with Ricci

*"Rhythm told Blues: I'll match you, Ace, I'll run
that rabbit all over the place. . . ."*

I SMILED TO MYSELF. Ricci would be comfortable in this gangster setting. I looked back down Waterway and decided that I could get a better look-see at the entryway to Le Sojourn which sits high up above the Hillclimb. To get there I had to climb what I call the "Moneta Steps," then cross the main arcade and go through the arched narrow walkway between a fish stall and a butcher's.

I started climbing and reached Le Sojourn's landing in under a minute. I was breathing hard as I watched the famous Seattle mist come in from the Sound. It was thick and clinging. Real city people wore it like a second garment—like I did. I held the damp railing and nonchalantly leaned over.

All along Waterway Avenue parking spots had opened up. About a block down, next to the auxiliary steam plant, a hooded, stooped figure pushed an overflowing grocery cart slowly up the sidewalk. I could make out the Riches Deli Market insignia on the side of the cart.

I smirked. "At least he shops at classy places."

His slow, purposeful progress reminded me of Hercules' little bug climbing up the tree. I knew that the sidewalk had plenty of cracks and potholes in it, so the figure had to be careful not to tip his cart over.

What had this beefeater sensed? Why was he coming home so early? I shivered and sort of lurched forward. I had to check myself. Just like on the ferry, I wanted to jump over the railing, to fly or fall like a stone.

I turned and went back through the vaulted narrow walkway. The fishmonger's shop was closing, but a group of men yelled out that they were from Fargo, North Dakota, and wanted to see some flying fish. They most likely had seen the act on TV. It seems every celeb on TV has thrown a fish.

As usual, Big Tuna, the fish stall's top manager, was outside the stall helping the group of tourists make their selections. Their choice of salmon ranged from fifteen to twenty-five pounds. When the order was given, Tuna waited till all the video cameras were focused on him, then he yelled out the order, alerting the weigher behind the stall. When the weigher answered, it meant for Tuna to toss the fish to him. Five fish were thrown and weighed in succession, each one heavier than the last.

Mongers always try to make the next customer buy a bigger fish, and it usually works out for the best for everyone, especially the mongers, because they're on commission. Everybody is happy with a little extra work after closing time.

I moved over toward the Atwater Produce Stall, the premier vegetable stall in the Market. Shu, the clerk from China, was storing his veggies in the cooler for the night. His trusty cat, Mecallico, was licking her chops. A greasy glob of fish guts lay in front of her.

I went around her carefully so I wouldn't disturb her dining, and walked down the little narrow steps where Rufus and his harmonica quartet played. There was Blind Spaghetti, selling his day-old *New York Times*.

Thank God.

I gathered my thoughts and focused on tonight's bit of theater. Blind was a serious concern. He was so honest that he might just spill the beans about the faked headlines. But I had to try.

I came up to him and looked him squarely in the eye. He was slightly snockered. He offered me a paper. I took it and checked the date. I smiled. It was only one day old, so that meant he was still good for a few more hours. So far so good.

I forcefully returned the paper and told him not to go away, that I would be right back. I hurried into Bugsy's and went to my office, unlocked the sea chest and carefully lifted up the bogus newspaper. I dropped the sea chest lid. It made such a loud noise as it slammed shut that Lea looked at me in a scolding manner.

There were only a few diners around, another good sign. The joint would not be so full when Ricci arrived.

With both hands holding the newspaper, I went back outside and gave it to Blind. I prayed that he was still sober enough to follow directions. Just as he took it, he spotted a svelte couple and quickly went to them, trying to sell my bogus paper before they entered La Gala. They didn't bite.

The club was one of the most expensive restaurants in the city, but Blind was tolerated because he sort of added the atmosphere of the alley. In other words, he was an authentic bum. Yeah, only in the Market are bums considered celebrities in their own right. Yuppies would get out of their sleek autos and feign fear of the dark alley as they quickly flitted into the establishment.

Several times a year a wild-eyed older drunk would navigate in a time warp, enter the chic eatery, and demand service. The doorman—Giraffe, as he's known around the Market—would gently escort the old codger back out and down the alley.

Giraffe is from the old days as well. Like me, he had metamorphosed, grudgingly evolving with the so-called new era of gentle hedonism. I remember him once saying that a person doesn't have to look like a bum to act like one anymore. It's a new freedom we have.

Focus! I reminded myself. I knew what my mind was doing; it was trying to get me to forget about tonight's activities. It was that old gutless side of my personality attempting to sabotage my plans.

I blinked, shook Blind's hand and grabbed my paper back. I explained that I was playing a trick on a friend who was celebrating his birthday, and I wanted Blind to try to sell my friend the doctored-up version. I showed the paper to Blind, and his eyes lit up in impish glee. I explained that this guy was as sharp as a tack, and to play it as straight as he could. Blind nodded eagerly and again took the bogus paper. Just then we were interrupted by two customers entering the place. Again, Blind eagerly tried to sell my bogus copy. Thankfully, they ignored him.

I scolded Blind and put the paper behind the ones he was carrying. Blind settled down some and got a bit more serious. He even apologized. When I told him I would pay him twenty bucks if he pulled the birthday scam off without a hitch, he showed a resolve that left me feeling somewhat better about the situation.

I left Blind, went up to the donut stall and bought a latte from Gretchen, who like most of the shop owners was closing for the day. I ordered a dozen powdered donuts, but she gave me three dozen instead, the last of the batch.

I took my loot over to Le Sojourn's landing and leaned over the railing, looking down on Waterway Avenue. The Dakota tourists had left, and Market activity was almost over. As I sipped my latte I watched svelte patrons of Le Sojourn stream in and out.

I liked the place when it was a wild beatnik bar in the Fifties and Sixties. Rumor has it that the great Jack Kerouac was a regular there when he was in town.

Back then I frequented jazz and rhythm and blues clubs along Manhattan and Hermosa beaches. I was underage—nineteen—but

I had a false ID. The joints had lined the Pacific Coast Highway all the way to the Hermosa Beach Pier and the Lighthouse, with Howard Rumsey's group. As far as I know, they may still be there.

I thought about my brief merchant marine stint during my Hollywood days, when I actually turned a buck. When I came to Seattle I went to Pete's Poop Deck, The No Place, The Penthouse. Yes, those were the class joints, I thought to myself. Up on Fifth was Gabe's. Best records on the jukebox anywhere.

Back then I had dressed up. Suits and ties and stingy brims. At the age of twenty I had been a regular at the bars. A big man in the jazz clubs along the coast.

I laughed; at least I thought I was. Today, every time I met a "legend" and tried to strike a memory chord, they looked at me like they had never met me. Well, they're all closed up. Haven't evolved like Giraffe and me.

It was a great life back then, full of hope and dare. I had hung around with Coldcuts and Tush. Tush remembered me, but Coldcuts refused to. Both are dead now, so . . .

So what? Got to make my own way.

Focus!

They had been the kingpins of cool jazz in the Northwest. Especially in Muscle City. Some dude in Oakland had called Seattle by that name way back when. When I asked him why, he said, matter of factly, "Well, like Houston, it's got muscle."

Coldcuts and Tush, though, were skin and bones from all the dope they smoked. Maybe I mistook the Oakland guy. Maybe he had said "smoky city."

I sort of chortled to myself. The guys had opened the No Place. It had been a pure jazz club. Plenty of berets, but plenty of stingy brims, too.

Tush worked on an easel behind the band. If my memory serves me right, he sometimes sat on a tall stool and worked with charcoal on newspaper, sketching the patrons. When he was done, he balled up the work and threw it at the subjects. His ploy never failed to work. The subjects would come up and beg him to sign the work. He would—but only for a price.

The joint was fun, with huge abstracts on the wall, and the fiery Coldcuts tending bar.

Well, one night in the early pre-dawn hours the joint's roof collapsed. It was good timing, because people used to drink there in darkness long after the place closed.

I continued reminiscing as though I were preparing to die: Dizzy at the Jazz Workshop on Broadway in San Francisco and here at the Penthouse . . . Brubeck at the Black Hawk, then later in the month here at the Poop Deck. It was funny: my merchant ship seemed to follow them on their circuit up the coast. I remembered seeing Miles and Cannon Ball. Saw Miles in N.Y.C., San Fran, L.A. At a party on a houseboat on Lake Union here in Seattle. Seemed like, in my 20s, I'd seen him everywhere. I was in awe of him, loved him and hated him. To me, he was the personification of the empty soul one day, then the next he was the richest soul on earth: All Souls Day, All Deads Day.

Well, it was a gas, getting emotional over a trumpet player. Where are these creative giants today? Dope did them in, dope and junk food. Same thing. I glanced down at my emerging fifty-year-old paunch and grimaced.

"Well, it still is a gas, dammit!" I said aloud. "Hey, I'm not farting." I felt my stomach, and it seemed flatter. Much flatter. I looked at my hands that held the bag filled with three dozen stale white D's.

Focus. A focus fueled by sex and fear.

I snapped out of my thoughts as a rage of anger swept over me.

"That's what focus can do, Dahlia!" I shouted.

I flung the bag of donuts out into the night. They shot out of the bag like a spray of bloated buckshot. As they landed, a flotilla of seagulls, led by Georgette, rose from their roosts and swept down into the blackness, their white wings flickering like ashes in billowing dank fog.

One "D" landed on a balcony, thirty feet out from where I was, causing a sleeping cat to jump two feet into the air. The door to the balcony opened and a huge woman, carrying a handgun, stepped out. She looked around with a mean, shoot-to-kill gleam in her eyes. Behind her the echo of an endless explosion of TV gunshots rattled into the night.

She looked at me suspiciously, as though I were about to leap the thirty feet to her balcony and force her to perform some unspeakable sexual act. I wondered if she realized how safe that balcony was, being five stories above the street.

The power of TV.

She spied the fallen D, froze, and looked around, suspiciously, like a kid thinking about raiding the cookie jar. She aimed the gun directly at the innocent piece of grease, then laboriously bent down and picked it up. The D just sat there in her hand as she held it up in the wash of light coming from her room. She looked at it closely and closed her mitts, looking up to the heavens as if thanking the Lord for this small bit of manna. Then she broke her trance, shrunk back into her normal slouch, and hastily retreated into her apartment, shutting the door. I heard three locks being snapped shut.

For a few moments I watched the gulls flickering above. Then I sensed movement below, and saw the shark snout of the Lamborghini glide into a parking place just beyond the Hillclimb sign. A damp Seattle rain had begun to fall as the fog got moister.

Seattle rain's so light you don't seem to feel it. You don't know when it actually starts. People are like fish in it. They just act normally. Seattle fishheads, high on droplets of fog . . .

Focus, focus, focus!

I forced my mind back to the job at hand.

Where Ricci had parked, just past the Hillclimb, was in a pool of frail light coming from one of the remaining street lights. It was a smart move.

I re-thought the situation: the phone booth was across the street; he would have to pass it when he returned to his car. I tried to make it out in the gloom but couldn't. I could see the elevator door below me on Waterway and knew that I would have to hurry to beat Ricci to where he would pass the telephone booth.

I watched him open the car door. From my drizzly perch five stories up, his sleek machine looked as flat as a pancake. I squinted to see if anybody else was in the car. Like Dahlia, perhaps.

My mind took off again, for I had the bright idea of going down to his car via the elevator while he was mounting the Hillclimb, then getting into his car with Dahlia and going off to . . . to . . . to where? Up Avalon? To the Luna Park? Maybe down to Cambria or a small Oregon Coast town like Florence? But then Ricci would have the keys on him. I thought of hot-wiring the Lamborghini with tinfoil from a Lucky Strike pack. No, no, that was forty years ago. A '49 Ford. She was a convertible. It was a dark night . . .

Focus!

I blinked back to reality. Dahlia wasn't there! Dammit!

She's at the Exacto, I thought. No, she's at The Grand.

Where the hell was she?

A knot twisted in the pit of my stomach as I watched Ricci slam the door, lock it, and cross the street. He looked up the Hillclimb and saw me, I'm sure. Big deal. I was just a figure in the night, a figure that was going to send him a message:

"I'm clean now, Mr. Solano. No guilt trips. She has no hold over me. Just take care of her, my man. And if you don't, you're going to get more of this."

My muscles were as tight as a freshly staved barrel. I knew I was going to beat him within an inch of his life in the phone booth.

Then I was going to carry him to his car and throw him in, like he had thrown Dahlia out.

He looked up at the city park that bordered Waterway, about a thousand feet up the street. Several cop cars were in rows up against the red brick of a crumbling building. Their flickering lights weren't all that unusual, what with the drug activity and street violence that occurred there at night. The whole park seemed to be taken over by aggressive street people these days.

A yuppie pick-up restaurant was up there. Its broad windows were tinted just like Ricci's car windows. The patrons of the restaurant couldn't be seen, but they could watch the antics going on in the park. Hmmm, petulant Neros and Nerolinas, fiddling with each other's private parts under the tables while Old Roma burned. The druggers were there because of the yuppies. The yups, to remain cool, needed the dope.

Yeah, ain't you cool, yups?

I looked up and saw two helicopters come swooping in from the north. From where I stood, the sound was a dull throb that blended with the stream of cars on the viaduct behind the buildings, unseen along Waterway Avenue. It meant that either a film was being made or there was an auto accident on the roadway. To me, it was just more background noise for the main event.

As I watched Ricci making his way to the first landing, I hummed "Hollywoooood . . ."

Hollywood had discovered the Market as a location site about five years before. Lots of films are being made here, I assured myself as I looked down on Waterway. It seemed that the helicopters were looming over the viaduct rather than the park, so there must have been an auto accident.

I heard still more sirens and looked up into the wet, murky sky for signs of smoke. I licked my lips to taste the dampness. No charcoal taste. I frowned. Those were fire engine sirens that stopped at the park. It kind of threw me. What the hell were they doing there? *Focus!*

I looked down again to check Ricci's progress and saw Curt, a market manager, emerge from the elevator and head for the happenings at the park. I knew his routine in the evening. He normally would have gone down the Hillclimb and across Waterway toward the waterfront. His favorite place to eat was there: the Don Carlos, a Mexican restaurant suspended in time at the Market. A large Enseñada family had brought it up, complete to metal tables and chairs and decor, which included ancient sombreros, 1920s license plates, brittle maracas, and a straight-line trumpet rumored to be from Pancho Villa's army.

I thought that if I pulled off the fried chicken deal with the Historic Commission, I would introduce Ramona's family to the Mexican family. I laughed at my word association ramblings. The Bianca "family" was the Mafia.

As I watched Ricci, I assured myself that the go-between was the white-haired lawyer, and Ramona knew nothing about where the money was coming from. Even if she did know, so what? The project was perfect for the Market. Saner heads on the full commission would see that. They understood that a major role of the Design and Review Committee was to make it hard on the applicants to see if they were serious about their dream of owning and operating a business.

For my part, it was a delicate balance. I didn't want justice. No. That sort of reality never happens in a society bogged down with too many points of view. I wanted Dahlia and Ramona to have a chance for their innate positivity to flower. I wanted the fried chicken shop to succeed.

I wanted Ricci dead.

I broke out in a sweat. I never thought I would wish that on anyone. I was being way too honest. Heat swarmed over me like a fever. My hot sweat mingled with the cold dampness.

I stood there, wanting Dahlia. My Paul Bunyan twitched.

"Focus!" I cried out.

The damned seagulls started flying again as if I was going to feed them a second time. I laughed at their greed.

I can't have Dahlia any more than Ricci can, I thought. He could possess her, for awhile, like a moth to the light. Until he was bored. When Ricci reached the foot of the last landing, he stopped to catch his breath. It suggested to me that he wasn't in as good a shape as he looked. When he started the last set of stairs I turned, went back and through the metal arches and down the steep Moneta steps, passing the management offices where all rents and money due were paid.

I call the steps "Moneta" after the street in Rome, on Capitoline Hill. There, on the left, stairs rise severely, straight up to what had been the Mint of ancient Rome—the Moneta. On the right is a gently curving roadway designed by Michaelangelo, a far more comfortable way up the hill, like gently curving Post Alley at the Market, the other way to Bugsy's. Post Alley was gritty, but it was a graceful climb. Old Michaelangelo would be right proud, hanging out down here with Blind Spaghetti and me. He'd be right at home with us contemporary artists.

Focus! Focus! I reminded myself as I entered Bugsy's.

Inside, in the warm atmosphere, slick pizza-dripping customers turned to survey my girth, then quickly returned to their gooey dinners. I had several twinges and hunger spasms, but gave my best Look of Eagles and focused squarely on Nan, the new dinner waitress, who was tuning up her sex machine for the night trade. She gave my girth a disdainful look: just a piece of market atmosphere, someone to wipe up or mop up after from time to time.

Part of the job.

Chapter 16

Prep

"When I saw her dancing with my best friend RAY!"

FROM MY CORNER of Bugsy's I looked out, thinking I'd see Ricci's car. But it was parked too high up Waterway Avenue. The hooded person had nudged his shopping cart another ten feet or so, moving slowly around the potholes and cracks.

I turned and surveyed my table. I didn't arrange my office; I didn't want a hint of familiarity if things went wrong. I was to appear to be a customer, that's all.

The new waitress was a big help because she didn't like me and it showed. I knew that when she spotted Ricci she would smell money and put on the hustle.

I still felt hot, and my shoulders started to tense up. I squeezed the edge of my table with my hands and murmured, "Deacon, just keep it cool."

I relaxed and checked my sleeve for the pack of loaded Pall Malls I'd taken from Tonk's truck. The hit sticks would play their part in my little drama, for Dahlia had told me that when Ricci got nervous they took an occasional hit from a joint he kept on the car's visor. Dahlia had told me that he'd asked her to buy some weed from her musician friends. It wasn't Tonk; she didn't know Tonk. Tonk wouldn't sell the stuff anyway: too much class. She knew Bondo and Jeeter, but they hadn't been around lately.

They usually hit the road for New Orleans this time of year. Tonk was just a musician . . . was . . . was . . . ?

Focus!

My hands had gotten all tingly, so I shook them vigorously. Well, Ricci would be plenty nervous tonight, considering the implications of Salvadore's disappearance. Maybe he would be relieved.

Hmmm . . .

I noticed the condiment tray in the middle of an unoccupied table next to mine. I took it and placed it in the center of my own. Between the sugar packs and salt and pepper shakers was a space where the matchbook was wedged in. I pulled it out and looked at it. It read "Bugsy's Pizzeria" and had a silhouette of a gangster aiming a machine gun. Anthony and Lea sure played up that old Chicago theme. I replaced the matchbook, tapping it lightly into the wedge so that it showed.

At the end of the bar was the cover of the Vivaldi tape I'd asked Nan to play. She looked over to me and I nodded. She grimaced and started to play the music. If the *New York Times* profile about Georgio Solano, Ricci's late father, had been correct, Vivaldi had been his favorite composer.

The door opened slowly, and I watched Ricci enter and look around. He just stood there for a moment, expecting to be waited on. His tight-fitting Armani suit was a bit puffed by the drizzle. His turtleneck exaggerated his long neck, and his black, patent leather Gucci shoes said in no uncertain terms, "I'm loaded." He was holding the felt-tipped sign I'd posted.

It pays to advertise.

I waved.

He looked at me like I was a piece of soft provolone, then came over slowly and purposefully. Diners' heads looked up at his magnificence, then bent down again to avoid eye contact with His Majesty.

"Well, I see you found your way," I said, getting up to shake his hand and pointing to the sign.

Instead of shaking my hand he handed me the flyer. I balled it up and flicked it toward the wastebasket: two points.

His skin was covered with a sheen of water. I wanted to believe it was nervous perspiration, but actually it was from the misty rain. Ricci was one cool customer.

He reached over to the bar, grabbed a napkin and patted his hands dry. His dark eyes darted over me like those of a young panther, warily and slightly out of sync. They were set wide apart in his skull and looked menacing, entirely devoid of compassion. I gasped inwardly when our eyes met. No wonder folks instinctively averted their eyes when he gazed their way.

He smiled ever so slightly, for he knew he had that effect on people. He cultivated that effect, I'm sure. But there was another hue about him as well, a slight touch of apprehension. Like how a robin feels when he senses the presence of a cat one minute too late. A suspended-animation kind of feeling. Like: What to do next?

I broke the tension by guiding him toward my table and holding his chair out for him. He liked that. In fact, he liked that a lot.

"Thanks," he said coolly, sliding snakelike into the seat.

"That's all right, Mr. Solano," I wanted to reply. "Mind if I call you Mr. Solano? It's about your late pop. For his honor. I hope you don't mind, but I asked for some Vivaldi. His *Concerto in D Major.* You know, the Largo. Yes, Ricci, it's a pleasure meeting your father's favorite. It's really a pleasure to meet you after all this . . . ."

What I actually said was simply, "You must be one of Ramona's sons. My name is Deacon. And yours?"

His smirk reeked of insolence as he arranged himself in the chair. He looked hurriedly at his watch, then rubbed his forehead.

"Roger," he said distractedly as Nan swished up.

She arched her hip tauntingly, then turned fully to Ricci and pouted her crotch in his face so hard I was afraid her thigh bones would desocket out of her pelvis.

He smiled, looking deep into her womb and then up into her eyes. His broad smile caused her to squeeze her bottom twice. Unfortunately, she had turned around and her female scent was wafting in the breeze. I had to do something because my Paul was beginning to stir.

"Why don't you try one of our local brews?" I said, a bit too loudly. Ricci nodded his assent, gave me a mean look, and turned back to Nan.

"The one I ordered is like an after-dinner drink," I said. "Thick and flavorful. TK is short for Thomas Kemper."

Ricci's eyes following Nan's arching rump as she tarted off to fill the order. "Man, all the talent in this market," he said.

He fell silent and squiggled nervously in the chair, as if to say he was in a hurry. "Just who the fuck are you?" he eventually asked.

I wanted to reply that I was the guy who had taken Dahlia away from him, but restrained myself.

"I'm kind of an independent go-between—between management and the people of the Market," I coolly replied, feigning seriousness. "Like if there's a problem, a leak that needs fixing, someone feels they're paying too high a rent—well, I step in. My pay comes from the deals I put together. Don't worry, I'd never do anything that would hurt the Market."

Ricci laughed. "Back east we have a name for your type. Ambulance chasers."

"Look Roger," I replied. "May I call you Roger?"

He smiled his approval.

"I know money when I see it," I continued. "I mean those plans. Ramona's lawyer, Mr. Sands, the way he was dressed, the way you're dressed. You've got to tell him that tomorrow when they make their pitch they have to dress down, wear a sweatshirt or something. Sneakers, like these." I raised up my dirty shoes and he grimaced.

Nan returned with our order and held out the check; Ricci ignored it. I filled the void by giving her a tenner and telling her to keep the change. She smiled her thanks at Ricci and ignored me. As she returned to the bar, Ricci's eyes again followed her rolling behind. Then he took in the place with a deep breath. When he expelled it he said, "Nice joint. Nice and homey."

"You from Chicago?" I asked.

He smiled, then smirked. "Yeah, sure."

"Great," I grabbed the menu. "Look, they got great pizza here, the best deep-dish in the city; you gotta try it."

"I haven't eaten," he said, giving me a grave, impatient look, "but I got things to do, so let's finalize this deal."

He firmly snapped his fingers, and Nan, as if waiting for the cue, came over. She bent over to hear his request, revealing ample cleavage. "Could you please change the music?" he asked.

"Sure," she said, smiling. "Weren't you the one that requested it?" she directed at me.

I looked at her while I drained my glass. How I put it down and answered her without choking I don't know.

"I don't mind," I said.

Ricci gave me a quick once-over. "You like Vivaldi?"

I was worried, because the hue of apprehension had deepened considerably.

"My sis was an Albinoni freak," I ad-libbed gamely, "and I don't like Grunge, Sinatra or blues, so since they didn't have any Albinoni, I picked the Vivaldi." I shrugged my shoulders.

A confused but concerned look came over Ricci's face.

"You're local, huh? I can tell you're local."

"Well, you might say that. I've been here a long time. Grew up in Santa Barbara."

"What did they do, throw you out? Ha, ha, ha!" he laughed, enjoying his joke.

I grimaced. Ricci continued laughing.

"Hey, did I offend you, big cat? Ha, ha! Local talent! You don't say! It can't get any better than this . . .

"Kenny G's local."

Ricci laughed louder. "Okay, Okay, have it your way. Put some Kenny G on, will yah, princess?"

Nan winked, stopped the music, and put on the dreaded Kenny G. Ricci settled deeper into his chair.

"That's better."

I pulled out the matchbook and toyed with it before placing it on the table. Ricci's eyes darted to the front door as it opened; I followed his gaze. I had a queer sense that Dahlia had entered. Like she had come up to tell Ricci to hurry because his car was in the process of being stripped.

When I turned back, Ricci was in the process of ripping the cover off the matchbook. He wedged an edge of the cover deep between his teeth. I presumed it was a nervous habit, so moved deeper into the deal.

"Look, Roger. This market is the number-one people place in the country. Millions of people come here to look for new ideas. Look at how gourmet coffee has taken off all across the country. Big, real big in Chicago. Well, it all started here. With what I saw of your people's plans in that meeting, you've got a natural. My offer to help is cheap, real cheap. Maybe I should raise my fee."

Now I had his attention. I topped it by telling him that it was a damned good thing he had shown up, not Ramona or her lawyer, because one of the Design and Review Committee members was sitting just four tables away. I gestured to a couple I'd never seen before.

He quickly looked in their direction, then just as quickly looked back at me. I detected a nanosecond's glimmer of hatred beaming out of his left eye, while his right one registered just a hint of boyish guilt, like one feels when they're spotted with their hand wrapped around too many free samples at the supermarket.

I seized the moment and held his eyes almost like Sal had held mine up at Les Troyans.

"Ramona looks fine, real good, authentic. The whole project is win-win. It's just that this market is owned by the public, so any deals have got to be done in secret so it doesn't look like anybody is being favored. Ramona's good the way she is. It will be a huge plus at tomorrow's meeting. Hey, the fact that a woman her age is trying to open a business is a big plus.

"Look," I continued unabashedly, "it's a question of finding someone that can turn the key. I can." I looked at him openly. We held each other's eyes for a bit.

"Like I told Mr. Sands, my fee is two thousand dollars."

He smiled and nodded. "One thousand now and one thousand immediately after the deal is passed at the meeting. Deal?"

I waffled. Did I really want this to happen?

"I certainly wouldn't go there if I was you," I stalled. "I mean, if that guy . . ." I pointed at my bogus committee member and winked.

Smiling, Ricci continued. "Ramona will slip you an envelope after the fried chicken concept is approved by the commission. If it doesn't pass, you will slip this envelope back to her unopened." Effortlessly he took a sealed envelope from his breast pocket and slid it across the table. I looked down at it without touching it.

"There are ten one hundred dollar bills inside," he continued. "Don't open it. You're going to have to trust me just as you've asked me to trust you."

I slowly shifted my left hand and felt the packet with my index finger, then picked it up and shoved it in my back pocket. My right arm hadn't moved a muscle during the exchange.

I took a gulp of TK straight from the bottle, still using my left arm. I felt as if I were a stroke victim.

He grinned. "A little nervous?"

"Well, yes, I'm a bit confused," I began.

"Confused? You get your price as long as you produce. Simple, no hassle. A sweet deal. Why should you be nervous?"

I answered with a question. "Care for a hit?"

"What?" He looked at me confusedly. Our exchange was like a tennis match, only he didn't know it, and the ball was in his court. "Jus."

He poured some beer in his glass in a purposeful but stiff manner and plunked the bottle down hard. He grabbed his glass and gestured with it. "Just what is this 'juice' you're talking about?"

That got me. Then I realized I had said 'jus' out loud.

"Lime," I blurted, as he was about to take a drink. "Lime juice."

He stopped. "What the fuck does that have to do with a hit," he asked. "A local blend?"

I pointed to the two lime wedges Nan had brought for us.

"Squeeze some lime into your drink. It'll taste better."

He looked at me quizzically and put his glass down. He expertly picked up the lime wedge between left thumb and index finger, then squeezed it with his right thumb and index finger. He took a drought.

"Hey, this is all right."

Nan sauntered over as I pulled the pack of loaded Pall Mall's out of my sweatshirt's sleeve. I smiled inwardly, for I felt I had slipped them out as smoothly as Ricci had pulled out the thousand gees.

Just two cool guys, sipping some microbrews.

My smooth movements were lost because he was watching Nan roll her fanny as she cleared a nearby table. When she turned with a wildly blatant cheesecake look, he smiled at her graciously and whipped out a thin gold pen and scribbled a phone number on the back of the chewed-on matchbook cover. On the front he scribbled the words "Bang! Bang!" cartoon-like, with arrows pointing to the snout of the machine gun.

She looked at it and laughed. Then she palmed the cover and tucked it in her apron pocket. The pocket was just big enough to hold one Susan B. Anthony dollar. I thought that she should have put it deep between her tits.

Mrs. Alice, I'm warning you!

I confess I was getting a little jealous. I conjured up that tune from the past, "Some cats got it and some cats don't. . . ."

Yeah, Ricci was one smooth character.

He looked at me as if I should tell him how macho he was. Instead I simply said "I thought she was going to wedge it between her tits. Maybe they're too tender from being crammed so tightly in her outfit. Maybe they should be set free to graze a bit."

He laughed indulgently, spilling some of his beer.

"Why are you so nervous?" I asked bluntly.

He looked at me, and for the first time the worry was clearly visible in his eyes. It crept over his laugh like fog over Telegraph Hill.

"Don't worry," I added nonchalantly, "those tits look tough enough to stop a truck. Let's have a hit. It'll seal the deal."

Ricci looked around, questioningly.

"This is Seattle; don't worry."

"Those are cigarettes," he said.

"They're doctored cigarettes. Doctored by Tonk, the guy who plays on the streets. Haven't seen him around today, though."

His smile was cryptic. "You don't say." He reached for one of the cigarettes.

"To Tonk," I said. "A master musician. You know, he writes all his own music. Jazz, classical, cowboy music. You name it. He is a gifted man." I took the exposed matches and lit his cigarette.

Ricci sucked in as if his life depended on that high. Well, he was going to get high all right. Tonk's sinsemilla blends are legendary for their immediate potency. His greedy suck continued as I brought the flame to my cigarette. If anything was going to go wrong, now would be the time. I didn't even smoke normal cigs, much less do weed. Shit. I closed my eyes, lit up and acted like I was sucking up the weed, which instantly brought back the taste of stale pipe tobacco. I coughed.

Ricci sniggered, exhaling. "Lungs of an old man" he said witheringly. He poured the rest of the beer into his glass, resqueezed the lime, then greedily grabbed my lime and added that to his drink. He took a swig and then launched into the cigarette again, taking another super gulp of weed.

Man, this guy is going to be knocked out in a hurry, I thought. I hastily stubbed mine out and told him that the cigarette was only tipped in liquid grass.

He watched me with suspicion, but it was too late; as Ferlin Husky would have put it, he was gone.

I checked myself: I was either getting a contact high, or else it was the real thing. The buzz rose as I looked into his eyes. No, no, Ricci's were dilating, sending me the message that his was the real high.

I stumbled to stand and said I needed some air. Ricci muttered that he would join me. We both walked stiffly, and I cursed my hyperimpressionable mind that I was actually getting loaded from contact. I had to get out of there and away from him fast.

As we made it to the door I saw Nan looking at us. Ricci waved to her in an exaggerated sort of way, then tapped his watch and looked at her leeringly. She smiled and waved us out the door. I wanted to tell her to skip it because he wasn't going to be in any condition to service her.

I hummed out loud, "Wang, dang, doodle."

At the doorway leading to Post Alley it really hit him and I had to hold him up. He looked at me in a disoriented way and called me a son of a bitch. He told me I didn't know who I was messing with. I assured him I did.

He looked at me, uncomprehendingly. Our eyes were no more

than ten inches apart. Hatred was trying to ride his bucking, swirling reality like a flea vainly trying to stay on a swimming horse. I know I had a smile on my face, because I was trying to wipe it off.

At that moment, Blind rushed over and heaved the situation beautifully over the top. To him, we must have looked quite normal: two sots out for a bit of fresh air. He came over, eager to share our high and, hopefully, the stuff that had got us there.

I nodded to him vigorously, but he didn't get the message. Finally, I just reached over and grabbed my *New York Times* from behind the stack he was carrying and placed it in his outstretched hand. Voila! After just a bit of hesitation he took it and shoved it right into Ricci's face, yelling "Happy Birthday to you, happy birthday to you!"

Ricci jerked upright, his eyes bugging out of his face as he tried to read the headlines.

"Happy birthday dear Ricci," Blind warbled happily, "happy birthday to youuuuuuu!"

I let Ricci go, and he stood there, spreadeagled in his stupor, just staring, unblinking, at the paper. Blind was really getting into it now and had started to sing the Happy Birthday ditty louder and in Italian.

As I edged away, I saw that Ricci had grabbed the paper and started to read it. I guess the headlines sobered him up a bit. As I cautiously backed inside and down the hall, I heard Blind starting to sing in German. Hell, he knew seven languages. This could go on all night.

I reached the elevator door and punched the button; it opened. I hurried in and punched the closed button and waited, looking through the door's slender crack. It seemed like an eternity before Ricci passed in his attempt to find his way back to his car. He was moving stiffly, like he was trying to flee rigor mortis. He stopped at the railing and looked rigidly down to where his car was parked, then took a deep breath and started to descend the stairs.

Chapter 17

Avenging Angel

"Felise Cumpleanos to you, Felise Cumpleanos to you . . ."

RICCI WAS STRUGGLING HARD to keep his focus. I sympathized. I hummed Happy Birthday along with Blind, who was still singing it in some language that sounded like Russian. I genuinely felt sorry for Ricci as he tripped and fell at the first landing. I felt an urge to leave the elevator and help him pick himself up. I almost opened the elevator, but a massive force overwhelmed me. It was like a host of spirits stopped me.

I'm missing something, I thought. My mind raced so hard that my loose synapses started vibrating. I mean, they actually were creating a sound in my brain like Charlie Mingus swinging away at his bass. Damn contact high! Mingus has been dead for years!

I sensed that the force was the same one that had tried to prevent me from entering Tonk's one-man band setup the previous night, only more powerful. I began to sweat.

A few years ago the same thing had happened by Morro Bay. I had been walking along the ocean beach when I was slammed to the ground by an unseen force—a huge oppressive presence weighing me down. I learned later that I had been walking next to an ancient Indian tribe's sacred burial ground.

My mind worked overtime, trying to remember. What was happening? The opening scene of the first Star Wars flick had tried to instill that same feeling in the audience. But, no, that wasn't it. That was just special effects.

Focus!

I realized I had no choice but to accept the force in the elevator, to follow through. Suddenly the contact high lifted. It was a clear focus now. On Ricci.

"See this through for my sake."

The command was so clear I whirled around, thinking Dahlia was in the elevator. Did I imagine it? Did she say it?

I started sweating again. I slammed my fist into my hand and flexed my shoulders. I looked angrily around the confines of the elevator, then hit the open button and stumbled to the railing looking for her. She wasn't there.

I leaned out and watched Ricci lurch down the next flight of steps. At the landing he turned with a jerk, his coat pocket snagged on a handrail. The pocket ripped apart, and the sudden release caused his weight to propel him across the landing.

He grabbed the railing, righted himself and looked up the stairs. His face had a look of panic. He stared up at me with eyes as empty as a live TV. They were popping out so hard I could see white around both irises.

He scratched his chin, looked down at his car, then back up at me. Judging by his movements, the immediate effects of Tonk's sinsemilla were lessening. Signs of normalcy were seeping back into him. He examined his torn pocket, brushed it with the back of his hand, then slowly continued down the staircase without looking back. Perhaps he was thinking that he had had enough.

But it was just the beginning.

I turned and rested my back against the door of the small elevator and punched the button for the ground floor, which exited on

Waterway Avenue. As the car silently descended, I felt the same sense of elegance I usually experience whenever I whoosh along in an elevator. It's a special treat for us ground-level types who rarely use them.

"The novelty is still there, Dahlia," I blurted out, hopefully, to no one. I felt an odd stab of pain in my side as if someone had jabbed me with a finger.

"That's not very funny!" I again blurted out, hopefully, to nobody.

I continued down, staring at nothing, flattened against the elevator door. When it opened at Waterway Avenue, I toppled out backward and fell flat on my ample butt. I quickly righted myself and again blurted out, "Okay, Dahlia; I get the message."

Again, I prayed I was talking to no one, for no one was there. I was angry at myself for falling, for talking to no one.

Suddenly I sensed movement. It was the hooded shopping cart vulture, standing—no, stooping—just ten feet in front of the Lamborghini.

The bug has arrived up the tree and expects to be fed.

Behind us I could hear the wacky tap dance of erratic shoes with what sounded like cleats. It was a pair of Gucci's, with hard, hard leather soles. I made a mental note of it since my shins were the second tenderest part of my anatomy.

I quickly glanced up at the landing. Ricci was descending the last set of stairs.

I squared my three hundred pounds of meat and potato-fed girth and moved like a fleet rhino—or, more accurately, like Oliver Hardy—to the concrete corner that Ricci would have to pass.

Us big guys sure can dance, Ms. Dahlia.

Ten feet up Waterway stood the vacant parking lot, anchored by the dilapidated phone booth which stood slightly askew barely six inches from the building's wall. Ricci's shadow appeared long before he did. I was just about to leap out and grab him when his shadow stopped.

I heard him snigger, then cough. It wasn't a cold type of cough, just a snort, a kind of clearing of the system.

The shadow silhouette again became animated, mimicking him when he patted his hair, then stooping to pick something off his left shoe. The flapping pocket was folded in on itself. It was as though the silhouette was preparing to depart Ricci's physical body.

I shuddered as the silhouette scratched its balls, then moved down the steps toward me. Its shape stretched and exaggerated itself like a spirit yearning for a higher plane. It grew longer in sudden jerks. I cowered at its enormity as Ricci stumbled down toward me.

FOCUS!

I swear it was Dahlia yelling. I looked around at the dancing shadows along Waterway Avenue. They were set in motion by the endless flicker of car headlamp rays blinking between the buildings as they flowed down the viaduct.

As Ricci made the last rung, his threatening silhouette deserted him and blended in with all the other shadows along the forbidding street. As he emerged, I moved out to confront him. He stopped suddenly, but his momentum carried him into me.

I slammed my knee into his recently scratched testicles. He doubled over from the pain, swinging his left arm in a wide arc toward my temple. I grabbed his hand and forced it around the edge of the concrete wall. I heard a rude snap.

I danced him down to the parking lot, turning him around three times as effortlessly as if he were Ginger Rogers. There, I wrapped him around the corner and into the phone booth with such force that the telephone receiver jumped from its cradle.

There was plenty of fight in him, but the element of surprise had thrown him off balance. I used that to my advantage and got him wedged into the back of the booth before he could retaliate. His head got stuck between the phone and the side wall. His eyes registered recognition of who I was because he was sobering up real fast. He had been set up, and he was realizing it. He started to fight back with all his strength.

"You don't know who I am, you son of a bitch!" he yelled.

"Oh, yes I do," I said quietly, pressing down hard on his supraspinatus, otherwise known as the neck muscle. I pressed harder and a strangled wail came out of his throat. He lowered his shoulders in pain and, for a moment, seemed to relax, shrinking down a few inches.

I was about to ask him some questions when I sensed his right hand rapidly moving upward between us. I grabbed it as fast as I could, for it now held a gun that he must have had strapped in an ankle holster. The telephone's automatic voice broke in . . .

"If you want to make a call . . ."

. . . just as I pulled his arm by the wrist, twisting it so that the gun's snout was tightly wedged into the soft spot just above his Adam's apple. I couldn't see the gun but it felt very small. Big or small, it added a whole new dimension to the proceedings.

I heard a siren in the background and wondered if someone had seen me mugging Ricci and called 911. Funny, it didn't bother me in the slightest. The gun sure did, though. I tried to think through what I was going to do next.

He yelled at the receiver, "Operator, operator! I'm being mugged."

I shut him up with another forceful full press of my avoirdupois against his one-hundred-sixty-pound frame in the confined space. It was no contest. Not even for the booth. Our combined weight shattered the glass rear wall, pushing us with a jerk six inches deeper straight through to the concrete wall.

". . . please hang up and try again."

I felt an electric jolt run through Ricci's body as if he'd been cut somewhere with a shard of glass. The smell of urine filled the air. Had he peed his pants?

I realized that the aroma was coming from the well-used patch of ground behind the booth. "Who knows," I thought, wildly, "Maybe even celebrities have relieved themselves here; maybe I should include this spot in my Market tour."

Focus!

". . . If you want to make a call . . ."

The siren was growing louder by the second. My time was running out. I glanced at Ricci. His face was less than four inches from mine, his head wedged behind the jagged edge of dirty glass that had stayed in place. The eye behind the glass was full of feral cunning, but the other, free of the terrible edge of broken glass, was staring at me in wide-eyed shock. It was as though his personality was beginning to break up.

I realized that I had to ask my question quickly or there wouldn't be anyone home to receive it. I felt a pang of guilt as I focused on the clear eye. Hadn't that been his problem all his life? Nobody wanted to deal with his evil side, so it was allowed to grow unchecked.

Well, I wasn't going to break the pattern. "Where's Dahlia?" I slowly asked him.

His eyes lit up in surprise. They looked like they were on fire. He arched his back with renewed fury. A thin line of blood appeared on his face that matched the broken edge of glass, enhancing his Jekyll-Hyde eyes. A laugh gurgled out of his mouth.

"What the fuck is with you?" he yelled. "She's a bitch, a fuckling, a junior-grade whore!"

The siren sounded just around the corner, up at the top of Virginia Street. I had to be quick. I pushed harder on his neck muscle and whispered to him, "If you ever beat up on her or ever mistreat her and I hear about it, I'll beat you within an inch of your life!"

He looked at me in astonishment. He sniggered and spit in my face, and tried to force the gun in my direction.

I pushed down harder on his neck and felt his body release ever so slightly. I asked his right eye where Dahlia was. It was swimming in a boiling sea of evil. I focused on the other eye. It was filled with pleading innocence, from a long, long time ago.

I sensed I had time to make one move, so I calmly reached down and replaced the receiver before his mind could come together again. Then I renewed my hold on his neck, forcing the gun even tighter against his throat.

"I want you to tell me where she is." I pressed as hard as I could.

"In a dumpster," he gurgled, his left eye registering a wary, guilt-ridden look, his feral one remaining a window into his malice.

My body spasmed. My teeth clicked together and I froze, dry as ice. Ice shot through my veins, streaked down my arms, through my wrists, and straight out the tips of my fingers, entering Ricci's body. He responded with a low growl.

"Where?" I intensified my grip.

"I don't know! I don't know your fucking town!"

The force reappeared and I squeezed harder than I would have thought possible. I could feel the force enter my arm at my elbow, ride through to my wrist, and spread into my thumb and fingers. My grip was so hard it felt as though my strength, and the force directing it, were interpenetrating Ricci's body. Ricci struggled helplessly.

"Pull the trigger," I said, very slowly and deliberately. Ricci's left eye looked at me pleadingly while his right eye remained as cunning as a cornered rat. Blood from his cut face was running down the edge of the glass in thick globules. It made me think of the borscht my mama used to force down my throat. I hated it. I repeated my demand.

"Pull the trigger. For Dahlia. For your pop. And for Tonk."

My right hand dug even deeper and I heard a muffled crack from the gun, silenced by my girth. The bullet tore upward and half of Ricci's tongue shot out sideways at least eight inches. The glass shards shredded it neatly in half. I thought I could hear the bullet ricochet three or four times, bouncing off the inside of his cranium and losing momentum as it sloshed through the grey sludge that had once been his brain.

His right eye, the feral one, exploded onto the thick plate glass like a bloody scrambled egg. His left eye popped out of its socket from the implosion. It still looked at me pleadingly, like a child who didn't know it had done something wrong. It was obvious that, for several seconds, it wasn't aware that the life had gone out of its body as it surveyed the scene from its new-found freedom out of the socket. Then it dulled, and I released my grip, stood stiffly, and regained my balance. Ricci's body didn't fall, that's how tightly wedged he was in the phone booth.

I glanced over my shoulder at the silent, hooded figure waiting in the shadows behind the grocery cart. At my feet were the remains of the seagull that had been run over. Nothing but feathers now. I jerked a look up Waterway as the siren pierced the evening.

I stood there, waiting to give myself up as the patrol car roared around the corner, barely a thousand feet away. It stopped and joined the line of other patrol cars. The cop got out and hurried into the park.

I went back into the phone booth and emptied Ricci's pockets of their contents. I left his watch but took his gun. I gave the corpse the once over, turned and walked toward his car.

I was about five feet away when I heard movement behind me. I froze and my hair stood on end. Grappling with the gun like it was a lit match, I slowly turned and saw that Ricci's body had become unstuck and, like a thoroughly dead snake, had slithered to the ground. At the same time I felt a sense of release, as though my synapses were relaxing after a hard day's work.

No thank you, no thank you, Spirit Rider. Shit . . . shit . . . shit.

I didn't want to ride spirits any more. I turned, staggered to the curb and vomited my guts out.

I always had taken the spirit-riding sensations for granted. Not any more. I was in the middle of Waterway Avenue, feeling empty, used, vulnerable, and as naked as the proverbial jaybird.

"Mizz Dee," I yelled out, "You take his spirit along with you, you wanted him so bad!"

I was as tired as I had ever been in my life. I was also alone and shaking from head to toe. No more spirits, please.

In a daze, I walked to the car, fumbled with the keys until I found the right one, then opened the door and stupidly held it as if Dahlia's spirit were going along for the ride. My hair stood at attention I was so confused. I was wiped out. I dry-retched.

She was gone.

Focus.

I sensed that the grocery-cart creature was waiting respectfully for me to leave. I slipped into the car. Instantly I was back in my old Austin Healy days. This was more elegant, but the lying down, the shifting—it was all the same.

I found the starter, and the machine came to life. It really did sound like a cartoon fart. I looked to my right, half expecting to see Dahlia in the flesh. I wanted to tell her about my Healy days, like the time I rode out to Malibu . . .

Focus!

The spirit thing had gone too far but I felt no remorse over killing Ricci, just relief, and anger at being used. But now I felt back in charge. I looked at the passenger seat, reached over and opened the door.

"Out, Dahlia, out!" I wailed.

In my primitive way I was trying to exorcise her from me, and to my surprise I sensed a cool kiss on my cheek. Still angry, I waited another second, then slammed the door.

"No thank you, Dahlia, no thank you," I uttered, to no one.

I eased out into the driving lane and headed south toward the ferry terminal. I passed the hooded figure. It didn't move. I looked out the rearview mirror a second later and watched it start across the street towards the phone booth.

I wondered if it was a professional beefeater. If it was, the only thing left in the morning would be some smudged bloodstains, a sticky magnet for gull droppings, lint, dirt, used condoms. The flotsam and jetsam of the day, stuck in Ricci's ugly blood.

I had heard rumors that if a corpse was fresh enough it ended up in the communal cooking pot down near the Kingdome. I shuddered at the rumor that the hooded ones carried the corpses through the underground train tunnels that ran beneath Waterway Avenue. Even if he wasn't a beefeater, most likely Ricci had gold fillings. Either way, the corpse would be gone by morning.

I drove carefully through Pioneer Square, following the confusing approach to the ferry terminal. The path was purposely broken up so drivers couldn't find it. Past Washington, left at Jackson, next right and then another left. Usually I just exited illegally on one-way Jackson Street, but this time I wasn't about to risk getting stopped by a traffic cop.

At the toll booth I lowered the window three inches and fed a tenner to the ticket taker. I accepted the change the same way. With the Hollywood windows no one would know who was driving the car, I reasoned.

I parked at the loading dock. As usual I had just missed the ferry. I sat there and watched the world from way below normal driving level. It fit my mood. It took me back to simpler days in L.A. and my Healy. My days of "stalking blood," as we called it, ever so innocently. It meant chasing women from bar to bar, not actually spilling blood. Like now.

Wow, I had absolutely no remorse.

Several young bucks who had started to mill around the machine gave me sidelong glances. They were animated and came over and kind of posed in front of the car. One greenhorn kicked the tires. He was strongly scolded by his buddy, who looked over at the driver's seat for approval. I gave him a silent, unseen thumbs up. The cowboys left, and I sat there unmoving, staring straight ahead.

I looked up at the visor and, sure enough, there was a roach wedged in it. No thanks, Ricci.

I looked around, fiddled with the small compartment between the leather seats. In it I found the registration and a manila envelope. I opened it. It contained three Polaroids of Dahlia in erotic poses.

Remorse and guilt both welled up in a rush. I fought the feeling as I forced myself to look at the photos. Normally, my ever-ready Paul Bunyan would have been inspired, but not this time. I thought that these must have been the photos the goons in the Market had used to try to find her. When I turned them over I was certain, for I saw that Ricci had marked the backs with her estimated height and weight. I remembered the goons' laughing when Ricci passed out the pictures at the cardboard box press on Pike Place. I now knew why the goon in the north arcade hadn't wanted the craftsperson to see the picture.

I slowly tore the photos into tiny pieces. Strange. Even though our affair never had the chance to get beyond the intense sex stage, I knew instinctively that was not the way I was going to remember Dahlia. I tore up the rest of Ricci's papers the same way. Then I rummaged through his wallet, using the Exacto knife on his credit cards and driver's license. I tore the fake cover off the *New York Times,* made a kind of folder from the paper's business section, and placed all the scraps inside it. The ferry announced its arrival with a heavy, deep, moisture-rich toot.

Very few cars are crossing to the island at that time of night and I was the first one in line on the dock. The deckhand directed me to the center lane. It was the only way I knew that the Bremerton ferry was operating on the Bainbridge run, since the Bainbridge ferry had four lanes down the center instead of just three.

Chapter 18

Climbing the Tree

"Somewhere, over the rainbow . . ."

THE OVERHEAD DECK LIGHTS went off as soon as the ferry left the dock, leaving me in the dark with only the steady, deep thrumming of the ferry's engines to keep me company. The muffled rhythms reminded me of a Gene Krupa solo on "Big Noise from Wenetca": Ta- ta, ta-ta, da-da, da-da.

I stopped humming and sat in the rumbling silence thinking about Dahlia. I reopened my impromptu newspaper sack and began to assemble pieces of the photos I'd torn apart. It was like a weird Picasso composition. I placed two arms together. A part of a leg. A section of her arm. Two pieces of her head didn't match. It was like trying to piece together a fractured memory. The more I tried to reassemble her image, the more frustrated I became.

I had sliced up Ricci's driver's license. I pulled a piece of it out of the scrap pile and turned it over. It was half of his face. One eye showing, his right eye. I must have sliced the card in duplication of the way I had last seen Ricci. Behind the jagged-edged glass, with the thin, bloody scratch running down his face. The eye, by itself, had a feral appearance about it. It stared at me. It was like looking at a miniature Ricci, safe but still nasty, like an ad on a tiny matchbook.

Staring at his bit of face lying there among the Dahlia scraps made tears well up in the corners of my eyes, thinking that she had been attracted to this creep. And the creep took her life, snuffed it out and discarded it like a container for a half-eaten eggroll. In a dumpster.

I rolled down the window, took a deep breath, and watched the dark, rolling water. The lights of Bainbridge Island were swiftly coming into view. I folded up the newspaper sack, opened the Lamborghini's door, got out, closed it gently and made my way aft.

Yakima-class ferries, which normally handle the Bremerton run, have a slightly different configuration than the regular Bainbridge Island-run ferries. Bremerton handles more walk-on passengers, so their ferries have less car-carrying capacity. Also, they're older, and their lanes are narrower.

I walked the length of the car deck. There are few cars aboard that time of night, and the ferry's metal walls vibrated from her engines, the whirring and throbbing propulsion sounds echoing back and forth between the tall bulkheads. The darkness enhanced the sound.

At the end of the car deck, I saw blinking lights from the city's office buildings. They sparkled like a diamond necklace nestled on a deep velvet pillow. I looked down at the surging water being chopped unceasingly by the vessel's powerful propellers. I thought of the many solitary passengers I had noticed on past trips who had stood in this same spot.

As usual, my first impulse was to jump into the water, to be carried away to eternity. Or did I just want to jump in and scrub myself clean?

I watched the flow of the water as it turned in on itself, creating a series of powerful whirlpools. I thought of the beaches in Southern California and how I had spent endless hours surfing when I was young. Perhaps that was the fascination I was experiencing. I wanted to surf in the *Yakima's* wake.

A wake for Dahlia . . .

I shook my head, sighed, and opened my impromptu newspaper package. I took a handful of scraps, kissed them, and tossed them out onto the water. I repeated the process until all the pieces were gone. I ripped up the newspaper, and tossed it into the water as well. I shoved my hands into my pockets, and watched the paper scraps twist in the water a moment, then disappear.

Unconsciously, my right hand fastened around the handle of Ricci's gun and tucked it deeper inside my waistband. I had to get rid of it too.

Suddenly I felt very naked. Just me and a four-hundred-foot boat, with maybe a thousand pairs of eyes staring at me from the passenger deck above. I felt as though I was on stage and any minute a spotlight would focus on me.

So I did the first thing that came to mind: I bowed and moved off, stage right. I walked against the wind toward the exposed side openings along the lower deck area. I had to duck my head when I passed the little lifeboat that hung on the side, one of two assigned to a ferry built to haul several thousand souls. Someone was optimistic.

At the side of the boat I was completely alone except for the seagull gliding along in the wind barely ten feet from me. When it saw me, it did a slight dip with its wing, and in a split second had closed the distance to five feet. It was expecting a handout, I presumed. I squinted into the night, trying to check the gull's wings, always in search of Israel.

I slowly removed the gun from my pocket. It was wrapped in Ricci's handkerchief. I unwrapped it and wiped it once more. It was a small .32 caliber. I held it at arm's length away from the ferry and dropped it gently into the Sound. The gull made a dive to retrieve it. It was so fast it almost caught the gun in its beak.

I studied the handkerchief for signs of a monogram. There were none, so I tossed it overboard, too. The gull gave its fluttering a cursory once-over, then ignored it and soared off into the darkness. The rag landed in the water, and for a split second its shape reminded me of the dead gull on Waterway Avenue.

As the ferry made its usual arc toward Eagle Harbor, I returned to my car—I mean Ricci's car—got in and waited to dock. I felt at ease, no more mongolopolase. I recalled what the word meant: spirits fighting with one another. It was an African word I had picked up somewhere. It helped me understand why my brain seemed to be always fighting with itself. I started getting uneasy just thinking about it. I always felt guilty about being at ease with myself. So damn unsettling. It made me nervous: goofy by day, then pay for it with nightmares at night.

A few minutes later other motorists returned to the deck. The overhead lights flashed on as we entered the dock. The first ones ringed the Lamborghini, singling it out for a few seconds before the rest came on. I was feeling a bit edgy. Would the cops be waiting for me at the docks? Had the grocery cart pusher phoned the police?

Two deckhands moved forward from right and left toward the ferry's loading apron to remove the ropes and direct traffic. Of course, I was the first one waved off. They paused just a beat, staring at the hundred-thousand-dollar car. Due to the tides, the departure ramp was angled slightly, but the low-slung machine managed to mount it without any problem.

As I drove up the roadway, I still half expected to see a squad car pin me down in its bright spotlights. That guilt-ridden thought expanded to include a ring of squad cars, with a division of officers poised with guns at the ready as I turned the corner onto Winslow Way. I breathed a sigh of relief to see that the street was empty—not one car was parked along its length. It was so barren it was like entering a whole different dimension in time and space.

None of the other cars made the same turn I'd made. They continued along the main highway, making a last dash to other island destinations—or even across the Agate Passage bridge at the north end of the island to the mainland.

The speed limit along Winslow Way is twenty miles an hour. Usually at that hour no one obeys the sign. But that night I did. If a cop had been cruising by he might have stopped me on suspicion since I *wasn't* speeding.

I continued past the little business district and turned up the street where Dutch lived. After I turned, it occurred to me that I'd solved the problem of what to do with the car. A tinge of that weird feeling, like I'd had at Morro Bay, spread over me. I warily glanced over at the passenger side. It was still empty. I drove slowly to Dutch's. Damn. The more I tried, the harder it was to control my actions. I was being directed again.

If the light was on upstairs at Dutch's place it meant he was home. If it was dark it meant he was gone. I stopped and looked up at the darkened window. I smiled and turned in at one of his many rutted driveways.

I crept in between a gutted '49 Pontiac and an old 1950 Ford pickup. Beside the truck was a 1956 Mercury that he'd restored. These deeply sculpted cars cast odd shadows from the past across my path. At the second pathway to the left, I turned between a 1950 Studebaker and a 1967 Ford station wagon. The wagon's hood was open and its droopy headlights gave it an appearance of a bulldog begging for food. At the next corner sat the remains of the Austin Healy. Behind her grew a patch of high weeds that had slumped toward the ground after my Buick Roadmaster had been removed from the spot.

I stopped the car and gently opened the door, leaving it running as I walked over to the patch of weeds. I pulled aside large clumps of Scotch broom. Thankfully, there were very few blackberry vines at this time of year. Once I'd cleared enough space I maneuvered the Lamborghini into the Roadmaster's spot. I turned off the car, took out a napkin I'd taken from Bugsy's and wiped down the interior.

Then I rolled down the windows and got out.

I looked in one more time to make sure the cockpit was empty. There was a balled-up piece of paper on the floorboard. I opened the door, picked it up and unwrapped it. It was the parking ticket Ricci had gotten on Pike Place two days earlier. I pocketed it, then moved around the rear of the vehicle and began removing the license plates. Once I had them off the car, I bent them in thirds. I would dump them in the Sound on my paddle out to the *Exacto*.

I redraped the weeds and scrub brush and stood back to admire my handiwork. You couldn't tell there was a car there since the Lamborghini was only a third the size of the Roadmaster.

I whistled softly as I retraced my steps to the road. I figured that in about twenty or thirty years Dutch's son would be walking through his inheritance and might find it. I looked at my pocket watch. Several hours had passed without my realizing it.

I made my way down to the dock where I'd tied up the rowboat. I felt exhausted and wasn't looking forward to rowing out to the *Exacto*. I stopped at the Roadmaster sitting regally in its parking spot. It was in a little field next to a communal garden. I rented the space for ten bucks a month. The car looked awesome after my short journey in the little Italian car.

I opened the door and spotted the sleeping bag I'd left behind the night Dahlia and I slept in the car. I got in and sat in the back. I'd rigged the front seats with bungie cords so they folded as far forward as they could go. My foot struck a hard, round object. I felt around and grabbed hold of a half-finished bottle of Bordeaux that we'd drunk a couple of nights ago. I remembered buying two bottles at Dahlia's suggestion. She knew about good wines. I fished around for the other and found it under the front seat. It was a dead soldier. My mind began splintering again.

Focus!

Was I going back to my normal self? A guilty, overripe, over-opinionated rogue? How in the hell was I going to digest the last couple of days' events? What the hell was my mind going to do?

Focus!

I wrapped myself inside the sleeping bag, opened the bottle and took a deep, long swig. The musty smell in the car reminded me of the night Dahlia and I slept there. How many times had I climaxed? Six or seven? Was I bragging? Had it happened? Bullshit!

I took another swig of wine and looked at the bottle's label. Excellent! Then I looked at the car radio, reached over and turned it on. It was set to an oldies station that Dahlia had picked. She said that the songs were still hits in the Arctic. Songs by Pat Boone—"April Love"—and something by the Chipmunks.

I slumped back on the seat and listened to the radio. It was an inane ditty I remembered from my teenager years: "Lolly pop, lolly pop, ooo lol-ly, lolly, lolly . . ."

I recalled my "years in the dark" as I called them. My last fifteen years in the Northwest. The land of the chainsaw and of the Puritan mindset, held in a state of total suspended consumeration.

I smiled and decided that this area was so cut off, so removed from the rest of the world, that it was totally unprepared for life in the fast lane. It's the Arctic Circle, in a way. Stay off the fast track. The real world. It's amazing. Flashes like Ricci come into town and foul up the neighborhood—killing, preying on innocent street musicians, driving flashy cars—and us local folks just walk on by, like the zombie beefeater who waited patiently while I beat Ricci to a pulp. He was a classic Northwesterner, patient and noninvolved.

Hercules would be proud of him. A noninvolved recycler turning the garbage of Ricci's body into an asset.

What happened to Sal's body?

My mind was filled by a vision of a beefeater unpacking his cart by the phone booth:

He removes an old 1940s-style radio. The cord leads down into the depths of his pocket to a battery pack. It plays Billie Holiday's song, "God bless the child, who has his own, who has his own . . . Mama may have, Papa may have . . ."

The beefeater pulls out a pair of white gloves and puts them on, like a surgeon about to enter an operating room. He looks down at the carcass. A rat looks up, a half-eaten eye in its mouth. The beefeater raises his head and removes the hood.

I stare into my own eyes. I am the street person. I pull out a big, fat, flat butcher's knife. It gleams in the moonlight.

I snapped to attention, my heart pounding. I was biting my knuckle so hard I drew blood.

My thoughts ran wild: Why the hell did she enter my life? She made me love her, kill for her. Now she will be with me in eternity. I'll never forget her. I know it.

I looked at my reflection in the rearview mirror that Dahlia had wiped clean. My eyes were burning with a gleam of fire. Bright and eager, like Ricci's. They were the eyes of a man who had boldly taken a life. I was sweating as I stared into my eyes, eyes like those on cops and murderers. I stared in the mirror and mentally flashed on the worst pair of eyes I'd ever seen, owned by Dave Devine, a fag who seduced young men for sex and hooked them on heroin. He transformed them into a gang, devoted to burglaries. Once they reached twenty they'd disappear. I knew he murdered them. All you had to do was look at his smiling cold-fish eyes . . .

The Roadmaster's right sun visor caught my eye. I noticed two rusted grips. I reached up and pulled it down. It squeaked. It must not have been moved in forty years. It revealed a vanity mirror. As I wiped it clean, I wondered why Dahlia hadn't spotted it. I shifted the mirror so that I could see my full face in it as well. I leaned back and watched my eyes until my mind drifted off and I thought about the power of mirrors.

What was that Englishman's name? The one who studied mirrors? Michael Aryton? Wasn't it he who said something about the toughest task in these modern times being defining reality and mirror reality? God, I hadn't thought about such things in years.

I looked at my eyes in the mirror again. They were back to their normal impish look. At least a nightmare hadn't wakened me.

Mirror, mirror on the wall . . .

That's how I found myself in the morning, looking at my reflection in two mirrors. I was still holding the bottle; I had drunk barely half of what was left. I took a deep breath, stole another peek at the mirrors, and stretched out on the seat. Outside my window the sun was just coming up. The radio was playing a silly song about not having any satisfaction. It had to be over thirty years old. That's a long time without any satisfaction, I thought. Only in America would it be cool to get no satisfaction for thirty years. This United States of Suspended Animation.

The radio jock announced that it was 7:30 a.m.

Something was missing. What was it?

No nightmare to review?

I leaned forward and turned off the radio. I rolled my shoulders a bit, yawned widely, opened the door, and stepped out into a field that doubled as a parking lot. I was stiff as a board. I took a deep breath and sniffed dirty smells.

I'd worn the same clothes for two days: socks, shoes and shorts stank like a Brady Bunch rerun. I shook myself and ran my fingers through my beard. Deep down I actually felt relieved, like a great burden had been lifted.

I looked over at the city that peeked up from behind the island's coffee roaster shack. The backdrop for the city's buildings are the Cascade Mountains. The sun had already risen behind them, and its cold rays shone on me. I couldn't see Miss Mount Rainier; she was behind the islands' southern hills.

I would have to wait for the ferry trip to see her. I had to see her. She was so reassuring.

I felt the envelope in my back pocket and ripped it open. Sure enough, there was a thousand g's. The Free Market Clinic would be happy when I turned it over to them.

The overcast had risen for a few hours at least. I was letting my thoughts get back into focus as I stuffed the money back into my pocket. It was difficult trying to separate fact from fiction. I tried to focus on Dahlia, but my mind wouldn't cooperate; I had to take a pee. I saw the bathrooms just down the hill in front of me, but instead used a nearby tree.

As I zipped my trousers, my thoughts returned to Dahlia. I looked at the Roadmaster with its rear door wide open. Kind of inviting looking. A jogger flitted right past the Buick and waved at me, flashing a toothy smile. I waved back and closed the door.

As I headed down the ramp toward my rowboat, I passed a couple of yuppies who stopped and stared at me as though I were about to steal something. I assumed it was my rumpled, slept-in appearance that gave them pause. The curse of Yuppydom is being uncomfortable with anything other than one's own kind. I remembered my Snickers bars and removed a heavily flattened one that had been in my back pocket while I slept.

"Please. For the little lady," I said, flashing my grandest smile and holding out the squashed candy bar like a cat offering its owner a half-eaten bird. The horrified couple turned and rapidly walked up the ramp. I stood there, my hand stretched out as if I were a statue, and watched them pass. The woman glanced back at me briefly, then hurried to their new BMW.

I laughed, ripping open the candy bar and eating it before I reached my rowboat. Yum!

The little dinghy was named *Priscilla* in honor of one of the women related to the late Elvis Presley. I didn't know which one: wife or daughter. The confusion was in the name Presley, for he always seemed to me to be both male and female in an odd sort of way. It wasn't a knock on the old rocker, it was just my personal observation. I ad-libbed an old Eddie Cooley song as I untied *Priscilla*.

"Oh, Priscilla, my sweet, sweet thing ya; let me put my arms 'round ya; now let me untie ya and take me to my boat—ya"

Getting in her was always a problem. She had a big, round bottom that rode the water high up. When you got in, she bucked and bobbed like a young filly being mounted for the first time. I put the oars in her locks, shoved off from the dock, and started rowing out into the still morning.

Just up the beach I spotted my rubber raft that Dahlia must have used. I rowed over, grabbed its line, cinched it up, and towed it behind me.

Chapter 19

Arctic City Blues

*"With a toothpick in my hand I'll dig a ten-foot ditch, and
run to the job of fighting lions with a switch . . ."*

I REACHED THE EXACTO without incident and glided along her purposeful hull until I reached the aft end. It's flat because a tug's tow lines have to come off her deck unobstructed. As I tied it up, I wondered how Dahlia had maneuvered the sluggish rubber raft. It was as awkward, in its way, as *Priscilla,* bobbing along on top of the water rather than moving through it. It was especially difficult for me, being as large as I am.

The *Exacto's* gunnels are rounded inward, so, to get my balance, I had to stand straight up while grasping around the thick wood hull. Compounding the maneuver's difficulty, I had to hold the dinghy's rope with my teeth. As I pushed myself up, the dinghy pushed away, stretching the rope and pulling my head down. To further complicate matters, Tart jumped up on my belly. Once I was stabilized I twisted around and slid aboard, hauling myself over like a sack of clams, my head hanging over the water. Tart sprang onto my back.

The boarding wasn't painful, just clumsy. If *Priscilla's* namesake was as ornery as my dinghy, I certainly didn't begrudge Elvis picking up any nervous eating habits from having to live with her.

Once the dinghy was secure, I righted myself and Tart and I made our way to the cabin. I looked up and saw Israel perched in the rigging just above my port running light. The glob of white birdshit oozing around the light told me he had been there for a few days. I smiled and waved a friendly wave, but that only scared him, and he flew away. It didn't matter 'cause I knew he would return.

I picked up Tart. Hmmm, she felt pregnant.

The cabin door was shut but unlocked, which was more or less normal, if it had been me who left it that way. But I was miffed that Dahlia hadn't locked up when she left. It was a simple situation. All she had to do was snap shut the padlock that was dangling on it like a flag, announcing that is was open to all the burglars passing by.

Man, I was getting catty. I mean, it was no big deal.

I entered the cabin, half hoping to see Dahlia there. I shook myself and made it to the head, where I ran some cold water on my face and looked at myself in the mirror. I looked different. Younger? Older? I searched each line and wrinkle and pore, but avoided looking straight into my eyes. What was I looking for? Whatever it was, I gave up when I smelled a bit of Dahlia, just a faint scent.

I froze for a moment, then began to towel my face dry. The scent was in the towel. Funny, it didn't arouse me. She was in my memory. She was an experience. I loved her memory like I loved all my memories. My Paul stayed cool.

I had a vague, uneasy feeling, but I didn't allow myself to slip back into self-remorse.

I replaced the towel and went down the tight little walkway and entered my galley. It was the best part of the ship. (I know I should call it a boat, but what the hell, it's my ship.) The galley was lined with wood shelving that held thick plates and cups and silverware. There was even a magazine rack. The tug had had a crew of eight when she was a worker. Now there was just me, so I had plenty of room, and I hadn't changed anything about the galley.

I moved over to the stove to brew my hobo latte. I brought the standing pot of water to boil, took the Half and Half from the stubby fridge, and placed a splash in a small copper pot, long stained from this repeated use. Next I added a heaping teaspoon of SBC to the simmering pot of water and stood over the two pots and waited. If either one of them came to a boil it would destroy the latte. At the right moment I took both of them off the stove, unhooked the strainer, and poured the coffee into an oversized cup. I added a level teaspoon of sugar to the hot Half and Half, unhooked the portable miniature mixer, whipped it into a stiff froth and added it to my brew.

Voila! Hobo latte.

I proudly examined the concoction frothing in one of my favorite cups. The cup I had chosen was yellow, with decals depicting South Carolina's South of the Border complex, Seattle's alter ego because its signature structure is a one-hundred-fifty-foot-tall Space Needle look-alike tower. The difference between theirs and Seattle's is that the top of theirs is a huge stylized sombrero. Ole!

I poured the dregs of the latte in a bowl for Tart, who, being a true Northwesterner, lapped it up eagerly.

I moved with my brew to my study. I had fashioned my study from what had once been the tug's radio room, so it was quite small. At the bookshelf I passed my hand over my complete set of Hardy Boys mysteries, but somehow I no longer felt so attached to them.

Yes, yes, the memory of them, or more accurately, the stories contained in them.

I've always liked mysteries and been attracted to them. Nancy Drew . . . the Hardy boys. . . . Dahlia was right. Why the hell didn't they ever meet? What the hell was wrong with the author. If she had met just one of the boys, and they had married and had kids. . . . I mean, why not? It was the same author. Hell. I decided right then and there that I would give the set to a charity.

Best live with the memory. Use the memory.

I looked over at my pile of Scrooge McDuck comic books.

Sorry, Walt, they gotta go too.

My eye scanned the tight, little room for other juvenile paraphernalia. I noted a stack of *Playboys* and a set of *Hustlers* next to it. Out!

On the wall I noticed last year's calendar that featured watercolors by a Market artist named Sarah Barber. It was frozen in time on the previous December, the month I had won the lottery. The scene was of the beautiful Market flower stand.

I took it off the wall and flipped through the months. Each scene was a world unto itself, just like the real Market. I decided to have each one of the scenes framed. I had to buy a new calendar.

I removed the old one, picked up a notepad and jotted down a reminder to myself to buy a new one. I paperclipped the note to the calendar, then moved to the next room along the passageway. It was my office.

I placed the calendar on the side of my small desk in a tray marked "Things to do." The calendar took me back to my duties at the Market. To watch over her and protect her. Why did I feel I had to protect and nurture the female? Like the Market. Like Dahlia. Was it because I was cast out of Eden?

Damn you, Mrs. Alice!

I slid open my desk drawer and methodically checked my stack of passenger tickets. Dahlia could have used one, 'cause I couldn't remember how many I had. I shut the drawer.

I flashed back to when I was being interrogated in Post Alley by the plainclothes cop, Jess Hallsey. That was one big piece of business yet to be answered 'cause I hadn't told him who I saw running away from the pool of blood. What could have caused it? Did Jeannie even know anything about it? I'd talk to Jeannie later. Above all, I wanted no more bad publicity for the Market. The blood-draining happened a full block away but would be labeled a "Market-area crime" by the damn media.

"That's right, folks, the drug dealer's blood was found just down from the Market's clock." That's the way the press always presented bad downtown news.

I passed the galley, grabbed some stale bread heels and moved aft and back out on deck. I reached up and placed the heel in the area behind the running light so it was unseen by the other gulls. Old Israel stood stoically aloft in the rigging. The slight morning wind ruffled his feathers just a bit. I was glad that the old bird had returned. Perhaps one day Tart and Israel would become friends.

Hah! Fat chance!

I gingerly sat down on my canvas director's chair and grabbed the cellular phone off its wall cradle, nestled just inside the aft cabin. I had to sit carefully because the canvas was beginning to rot. Damn, I thought, I wish I had someone with me to share the upkeep. Maybe I should hire a maid.

Once ensconced I surveyed the city seven miles distant. Between us, Puget Sound shimmered with a mosaic of three million different reflections of the morning sun. I dialed the Seattle Police Department.

A pleasant-sounding woman answered and I asked for the Missing Persons Department. After a pause, a gruff voice announced.

"Craig here."

"I want to report a missing person."

"Name?"

"Dahlia Swartz."

"You don't sound female."

"Dahlia is the one missing, sir. She's about twenty-three to twenty-five years old."

"Your name, please."

I held my breath and pressed on. "Look, I want to remain anonymous. I believe the young lady was murdered two nights ago."

"Oh, is that right? Anything else?"

I was totally blown away by his bored attitude, as if these reports came in all the time.

"Yes, there is something else. I also believe a Market musician was murdered about the same time in the parking lot under Market Park. His name was Tonk, and they both ended up in a dumpster."

There was a long pause, then Officer Craig said bluntly, "Do you know the Totem Pole Climber?"

That really threw me.

He repeated harshly, "If you do, and you're putting us on, you gravely risked the poor man's life. Now, who are you?"

I quickly hung up. What the hell was he getting at? I remembered that a call can be traced if you don't make another one quick, so I dialed Information and asked for the garbage company. I dialed the number they provided, and another pleasant secretarial voice answered. I asked for the boss, but the voice kept on talking. It was a digital recording and spooky in that it sounded so real. It told me to push some buttons. I pushed the three button and a guy's voice said "Bill Desens here." I immediately pressed to the heart of the matter.

"Bill, I suspect that two friends of mine ended up dead in your dumpsters a couple of nights ago."

I waited for his response, but there wasn't any.

"Sir, I'm serious. I believe both were murdered."

"Eh, mister, say that again. . . ."

I repeated myself, and he answered in a concerned voice.

"Look, I believe your first step should be to call the police."

"I did. They hung up on me."

He lapsed into a kindly delivery and said, "Look, if the police hung up on you, what should I do? What do you want me to do?"

"Check your goddamn dumpsters for starters."

"All of them? We must have ten thousand! Look, I'm trying to be helpful, but . . . . Where were they dumped?"

"I don't know."

"How were they supposed to have been killed?"

"I guess with a cobbler's hammer."

There was a long pause, followed by a nervous cough.

"Look, my advice to you is to see a professional. Now, please don't take this personally. I promise to look for any bodies, but most pickups and removals are tightly scheduled. But please: See a professional. Good day."

I held the phone . . .

He didn't hang up either . . .

"Look," he continued, "if any of this ends up in the paper, whoever you are, I'll find out. I'll sue you for everything you have."

He hung up with a firm click.

Man, I was getting nowhere fast. I talked into the dead phone.

"Look, you don't know me but I just killed a guy last night because he killed my girlfriend. Yes, he also had a hand in killing a talented musician and countless other people, including his own father. Please call the cops. I don't even know if the body is still around because the beefeaters were hovering. Yes, that's the street name for cannibal grocery-cart street people."

I stopped talking and held the phone for a full minute, seething with anger, then threw it in the Sound. I turned and walked back into the cabin toward the galley.

Tart was still slurping as I sat down and took a notebook out of the magazine rack and began to draft a public notice.

"To the parents or relatives or friends of Dahlia Swartz, formerly from a community inside or near the Arctic Circle. Dahlia disappeared in Seattle this month. Her whereabouts are unknown. . . ."

I stopped. What else could I say? Was she really from some-where above the Arctic Circle? Also, Dahlia had said she had gotten her name from the crime film that starred George Raft as a priest who cultivated dahlias. Ten to one it wasn't her real name.

I continued with a description. "She had grey eyes, was about five feet three inches tall, on the skinny side, and was blond and sexy." I scratched out "sexy" and wrote "vivacious." Then I crossed that out and wrote "precocious."

This was going to take some doing.

In the magazine rack was a world atlas. I brought it down, opened it, and studied the Arctic Circle. There were only a few place names. I made a mental note that when I got a final draft of my let-ter ready I would go to the downtown library and get a more com-plete listing of Arctic Circle communities.

Shit! Had Tonk been right after all? Was Dahlia really from Massachusetts? Or Arizona? Or Kansas?

I slipped my draft inside the atlas and sat there with my cup of joe. My mind wandered to Ramona and her fried chicken shack con-cept. That brought time into sharp focus, and I glanced up at the clock. Till then, food had been as far removed from my consciousness as I would be from a Congregational Church picnic.

I mean, I just wasn't hungry. Man, that was a switch. It was al-ready 10:00, so if I hurried I could get the 11:10 ferry, get to the li-brary, do my research and make the Historical Commission meeting.

I removed my rumpled clothes and headed for the shower. On the way I stepped on the scales and about jumped out of my skin. It said I had lost ten pounds since A.D—since "After Dahlia."

"I just wasn't hungry," I muttered.

Maybe I was reentering the human race. I mean, I'd never left it, but . . .

I stepped into the hot shower and lathered down with Dial, scrubbing as hard as I have ever done. My scrubbing seemed to release all the aches and pains of the last days. My ear stung where the goon had grazed me with the cobbler's hammer. My legs were stiff from being cramped up in Henrietta for the night. All my muscles were aching from using them so forcefully on Ricci.

I had killed a man . . .

Focus! No self pity!

I turned the shower off and watched all the hurt and dirt and guilt slither down the drain. I stepped out, turned and looked into the mirror. I saw just a shadow of my old self outlined in the mist from the steaming water. I took the towel, wiped it clean and looked directly into my eyes, man to man. Or should I say, man to reflection? I had changed, but was I looking at that somebody I had always thought I was? I mean, who else?

No, that was bullshit! I concentrated deeper and looked at my reflection again for a solid ten minutes. Then I slowly lifted my index finger and touched the mirror. The reflection did exactly the same. Our fingers touched right at the surface of the glass. I shifted into my reflection.

"No more mongolopolase," I mouthed slowly, from inside the mirror, watching my physical body repeat exactly what I said at the exact moment I said it. I placed my other index finger on the glass, this time initiating the act from the mirror. My physical body's finger met mine.

"We are both one now, okay," I told my physical self. "And I mean together for once in our life. That means no more clowning around, right?" I felt my spirit return to my body. I and my reflection initiated a smile.

"Yes, Dahlia Swartz," we said in unison. "May her spirit rest in peace. It was she who brought me together."

Chapter 20

Hercules Re-Revisited

"Would you like to go riding in my Buick '59,
Buick 59, Buick '59? Ooooo . . ."

I MADE IT ACROSS Eagle Harbor in Priscilla without incident, but had to hurry to make the ferry because I had forgotten that my scooter was still at the Market. I had wanted to scoot past Dutch's to see if the Lamborghini was completely hidden, but that would have to wait.

As I walked, suddenly all Dahlia's verbal ramblings of the past few days burst out of my memory banks and I began to piece together what I knew about her.

She said she had run off with a serviceman. A guy from the Army, I think.

Or was it the Air Force?

They flew down to Chicago, and he tried to take her home to meet his folks in Toledo.

Or was it Akron?

But they wouldn't let her in the house. She said she must have looked like a little rat, because she had borrowed a big-shouldered friend's fur coat that was three times too large for her. The guy . . .

Did she say his name was Jake?

. . . ran out of money and disappeared, and she got kicked out of the motel. She said she had blow-jobbed her way to Minneapolis with a tractor salesman, then a wholesale shoe supplier whose van smelled like stale shoe polish. At a mall just outside the city she met a group of street musicians working on their old bus.

They were from Greenwich Village and were heading west to Seattle. She hitched a ride, and all was well and free-loving until Butte, Montana, when the bus gave out for the tenth time. The guys worked on it and got it ready to run, but the battery wore down. She said it was the funniest sight from the rear because it was a big bus, and all these wildly dressed people were pushing it. Once it started moving, it was easy, she said, because the bus was actually at the start of a long highway decline, so all they had to do was get it rolling. She said that when it got going fast enough, all the people jumped aboard, but she stumbled just as the bus rounded a curve. It was out of sight when she heard it start by compression. The driver didn't see her fall, and she was stranded again. She said she was really scared because she had absolutely no idea where she was.

About ten minutes later Ricci showed up in his fancy car. She described his arrival like he was some sort of saint in a cloud of dust. "Kind of like you did," she had said coyly.

She said that Ricci was like a sex demon, possessed, and needed her sexually practically every other hour. She said they would stop in the empty land and just get it on standing up. Once, on a hill by the river, they pulled over, and she mounted him in a thicket. The road swooped around in a hairpin, and one alert driver beeped his horn in appreciation of the unexpected roadside attraction. She said they went to more than twenty chicken ranches across Idaho, Montana, Oregon and Eastern Washington, spot-checking the take from the cock fights. She had been with him almost a month.

She commented that one day they were completely in love, and the next he was backhanding her. The backhandings got stronger. I recalled her mentioning that he got a call that made him really tense, almost frightened. The next thing she knew, they were in Seattle and had got a room at a fancy hotel.

The Grand Hotel.

It was three days later that I had found her. She had mentioned that Ricci had demanded she find the bus hippies and get some grass. She didn't find the guys, but she scored at the Market.

Let's see . . . was that all?

A thought surfaced. No, she did mention meeting a suave, grey-haired guy. Mr. Sands? It couldn't have been Salvador; he wasn't slick. Neither were his two goons. Had to be Sands. The Mafia wanted Ricci to oversee Ramona's fried chicken shop idea in the hopes that it would be successful, and Sands was the link between the legit (Ramona) and the dirty money. It fit.

The last piece of the puzzle. Ricci's father Georgio was a pro at laundering money. What a perfect plan, to launch a chain of fast-food outlets based on the one designed for the Market.

Where did Salvador and the goons come in?

Okay, I got it: Ricci was horny because he had laid off women on orders of the bosses. He was exiled from the East Coast. Had to have been; he was too well known. His actions broke his father's heart. The big boys just didn't want him around until the heat died down. So they shipped him out west to monitor chickenshit.

Somewhere along his route of checking on chicken ranches and cock fights, word got back east that he was messing around with a young girl—again—and Sal was sent out to squelch the affair. Judging by Ramona's plans for the shop, the hoods were banking heavily on the deal going legit and wanted no screwups.

Tonk? The goons thought he knew something about Dahlia. Obviously Salvador knew Tonk because, after the Aerostar was damaged, he was taking me down to Tonk's van. I shuddered.

Thank God for CNN.

I mused: They killed Tonk and Ricci killed Dahlia. Herc killed Sal and I killed Ricci.

"What the hell," I said, shrugging my shoulders. "Two eyes for two eyes." Ah, the shit of it all. I had saved them the trouble of getting rid of Ricci once Ramona's plans were realized.

I was one of the last passengers to board the ferry as it tooted its one-minute-departure warning signal. I strolled forward through the massive double-ender up to the galley, on the Seattle end. I took a seat where I could watch the other passengers and thought about the differences between ferry runs.

The first run of the morning is the best. The 5:35. On that run, all walks of life mingle and respect each other's space. Not a jostle or a sneer in sight.

A vastly different crowd rides at 7:10 and 7:50. These hustling, bustling commuters are the wanna-bes and can-doers of lower and middle management, plus a gaggle of lawyers who practice harsh postures on the smattering of blue-collar commuters. Maybe they resent having to share the ferry with folks from the lower rungs of the economic ladder. Or maybe I'm just reading into it; maybe that's the way they are all the time.

The late-morning riders—like the ones I was looking at—consist mainly of corporate heads, retired folks, and a large contingency of housewives and mothers heading to the city to shop.

As I looked around I realized I knew far too many faces. I'd probably served them all at one time or another. A lot of them come up to me on the ferry, asking the price of watermelon or artichokes. Interrupting a person's countenance on a commute is totally taboo, but I actually didn't mind. I loved talking about the Market.

I remember a well-meaning commuter who ran for office. Her campaign consisted of going person to person as the ferry made its way to and from the city. Even though she was well liked, she lost big time. She broke the taboo.

I saw Sam Read, a long-time commuter, a class guy, and we exchanged nods. He looked like he wanted to talk, and I knew he was giving me the courtesy to settle down before he came over. The morning's P.I. was draped over his crossed legs. There was a large photo on the cover. It gave me a queasy feeling. Had Ricci's body been discovered?

I joined the line in the galley and ordered an egg on an English muffin. The gal gave me my number. I moved up the line and got a Starbuck's, then paid the cashier. I felt sort of guilty drinking from a green cup rather than my SBC red, but in a pinch . . .

I went over to an empty table but passed it up because of the catsup glob in the middle. Perhaps the blob of red had attracted me to it, but I forced my mind to ignore it. As I was about to sit down at a clean booth, my number was called, so I went back and picked up my egg-on-a-muffin. I had noticed that the cook was making a batch of sandwiches so I knew it was fresh.

I returned to my table, set my breakfast down, picked out thirty-five cents change, and walked over to the newsrack to get a paper. I was nervous as hell. For once didn't want to read it. But, well . . .

There was something vaguely familiar about the cover pic. I caught glimpses of it through the small line in front of the vending machine. As I waited my turn, I looked out a side window and saw my Miss Mount Rainier in all her splendor. She wasn't as pretty as when you see her topside early in the morning, with the sun just rising, but her presence was reassuring. I counted seven gulls starboard; that's a lot of gulls for one cross-sound trip. Then I saw why. Lots of kids were throwing bread scraps for them to catch.

I put my change in the machine, pulled out a fresh copy, and stared into the face of Hercules looking up into the picture from on top of one of the Market totem poles. I just about lost my sealegs.

I hurried back to my seat and started to scan the article.

"Market fortune teller climbs Market Park totem pole." I began

reading: *"Hercules, a well-known Market personality, was reported last night to have been seen throwing a large bag over the ramparts of the park. An unidentified caller described the bag as looking as though it might have contained a human body. Police immediately arrived at the scene and Hercules attempted to run away. Finding himself trapped in a circle of advancing police officers, he climbed the totem pole. It took officers four hours to get him down from his perch. Hercules is noted for the peculiar garment he wears—a dashiki covered with Barbie Dolls. He had torn Barbies from his garment and tossed them at the circling helicopters. Hercules, true to his name, heroically resisted rescue efforts for hours. But he eventually tired, and a search and rescue officer was lowered to the top of the pole, and was able to strap a harness around the six-foot-eight-inch man. He was lifted to safety and is now under intensive care at Harborview Hospital.*

Officers found no trace of a bag, large or small, said by the witness to have been thrown from the park. Police questioned the witness, who was later released. Hercules has a history of medical problems, and charges may be filed against the young lady reporting the incident for "reckless endangerment" to the unfortunate giant.

So, that's what had been happening at the park just a thousand feet from my little drama. Well, the beefeaters must have snagged another one. Yuck! The last place to look for truth is the papers!

Then it came to me: Ah, ha! So this was why the Missing Person's officer, Craig, wanted to know if I knew who the totem pole climber was . . .

I scanned the paper thoroughly for any article pertaining to bodies found in or out of dumpsters. There were none. There was a small report in the "local" section about the knifing of a drug dealer in Dope Dealin' Alley—down by the Market. Shit! Just a paragraph. A kid with a street name of Jerk, age fourteen. The article reported that he had a long history of drug-related arrests.

A thought thrust forward. Maybe Tonk wasn't killed. Sal didn't say he was dead, just in a dumpster.

Hmmm. Tonk once spoke up for a cause at a Market meeting. Later he had that look of fear that maybe he had said too much. He disappeared for three months after the meeting. But how to explain his truck being there? I made a mental note to check his truck again.

Sam came over with his copy of the paper.

"How do you like that? You guys at the Market sure know how to pull off PR stuff."

"Well, he could have fallen," I answered curtly, "and we all would have lost a good seer."

Sam understood. "Yes, I know. He has a booth down on the lower level, doesn't he?"

"That's the one.

"Would he kill someone?"

"Come on, Sam!" I laughed. "Nobody is killed at the Market. That's the friendliest place in the world. Has to be with all the commerce going on."

"Hey, you don't have to sell me," he replied.

But I continued trying to hide my guilt. "I mean things happen around the Market, and the Market gets the blame. A robbery could take place eight blocks from the Market, and it will still get the blame. That's the down side of being considered the heart of the city."

Sam continued to bait me. "Well, you've got to admit that there are a lot of weirdos down there."

"Not weird, just colorful individuals expressing themselves."

"You can say that again. Where are you going?"

"To the Market."

We both laughed.

Epilogue

J UST WANT TO TIE UP some loose ends. It's been over six months now since being with Dahlia, and it all seems more and more like a dream. Not surprisingly, no one from inside the Arctic Circle has responded to my queries about Dahlia. As for my "commission" for my part in the deal—well, it bought the Free Market Clinic some much-needed medical supplies.

On reflection, I understand why Ricci murdered Dahlia: to save his own skin. He knew the Mafia simply wouldn't tolerate another scandal with him at center stage. By killing him I had simply done the Mafia a favor, getting rid of an embarrassing Neanderthal throwback. I had also helped them by greasing the wheels to get Ramona's business plan approved.

High fives are due the Pike Place Market, that grand old lady whose magic in fostering new businesses proved itself once again: Ramona's Fried Chicken Shops were an instant success. I read in the papers that they've just opened a third location in Missoula. Not surprisingly, it's still a closely held private corporation. The article also mentioned that they're changing the name to "Chicken Jive Inns." Great move. Seems like I already know the name, somehow.

Mr. Singe, the Market's manager, finally answered my call with a letter. He wrote that Mrs. Sanchez couldn't be allowed to sell her aprons on the day-stall tables because she wasn't hand-making them; she wanted to use a sewing machine. I fired back that the rules should be bent for her because she was in her seventies, had a problem with her sight, and barely spoke English. I added that keeping her out of the Market would be denying Seattle customers the opportunity to purchase a unique Philippine-designed product.

I also added—tongue in cheek—that I supposed he *might* have a case against keeping her out. Might have, assuming she was fronting an army of three thousand Filipino seamstresses, who were sitting at banks of sewing machine work stations on board a re-vamped, decommissioned aircraft carrier, anchored in international waters off Washington state, and poised to take over the apron industry of Seattle. But in actual fact, she was just a proud senior citizen, who simply wanted to remain productive and independent.

Not surprisingly, he still hasn't given me an answer.

I find his treatment of her an outrage.

Hmmm. A letter to the AARP might help.

After all, aren't I Deacon Davenport, Fishmonger Emeritus of the Pike Place Market?

Author's Note

Popular music from the late Forties and Fifties is an integral part of Deacon's psyche, whether hard-driving R&B, celebrative R&R, or popular tunes. In particular, Deacon loves what might be called a "lost" era of American music: during and just after World War II when there was a shortage of metals used in musical instruments—brass in particular—due to the war effort. Not to be stopped, musicians created wonderful a capella arrangements that used the human voice in innovative ways.

The lyric excerpts at the beginning of each chapter are from the following songs, listed in order by chapter. Examples of songs influenced by "lost era" music are indicated by an asterisk.

About the Author

Michael Dovell is a founding member of the "Ambler, Chandler and Himes Club," for which the only membership requirement is to have this trio of writers in one's bedside library. Needless to say, these three are his favorite mystery writers, along with Dick Francis and Earl Emerson.

Born in Washington D.C. in 1941, Mr. Dovell is a descendent of Huguenots who settled in the Shenandoah Valley in the early 18th century. At seventeen, he joined the Navy to see the world. Since this only whetted his appetite for travel, he followed this with a stint in the Merchant Marine, then land duty in Southern California, New York City, London, Rome, and Spain. Mr. Dovell now lives in Seattle. This is his first novel.